RUNAWAY MINISTER

As a child, **Nick Curtis** was addicted to police procedurals on TV. He dreamed of joining the police force, but actually started his career as a civil servant! Now he divides his time between his family, restoring his beloved MGB Roadster and creating his fast-paced political thrillers. Nick lives with his wife and two children in the Dorset countryside.

RUNAWAY MINISTER

NICK CURTIS

BLACK STAR CRIME™

First published in Great Britain 2008
Black Star Crime
Eton House, 18-24 Paradise Road, Richmond, Surrey TW9 1SR

© Working Partners 2008

ISBN: 978 1 848 45000 4

Set in Times Roman 10¼ on 12¼ pt.
081-0908-60222

Printed and bound in Spain
by Litografia Rosés S.A., Barcelona

With special thanks to Graham Edwards

Prologue

March 1st
09:35
Croatia Airlines, Flight OU 312

THE CABIN crew made their way down the aisle, collecting empty meal trays. As they moved, the cheap fabric of their uniforms rustled against their legs. It was funny, Javor Milos thought, how the airlines made so much effort dressing their staff like soldiers.

Milos wondered how the crew would cope if someone pulled a gun. They were trained, he supposed, but they weren't prepared. Not that guns were Milos's style, not any more. He certainly wasn't stupid enough to try and smuggle one on board. Nor was he about to blow the operation by going berserk at thirty thousand feet. Going berserk wasn't his style either. Patience was. He'd waited over thirteen years for this. He wasn't about to destroy his chance of revenge for the sake of another hour or two.

A blonde stewardess took Milos's tray. She had to lean over him to reach the tray of the man in the window seat. Her hair smelt of apples.

'How long until we land?' asked Milos.

'Not long now, sir,' said the stewardess. Her smile was bright and plastic, like the food. 'The captain will be making an announcement shortly.' She moved on, brisk and disinterested.

Milos looked past the stranger beside him, through the little window, out across the wing of the Airbus. England was lost beneath a still sea of cloud. As Milos watched, the plane dropped towards the cloud. Tendrils of vapour started streaming past the window. The Airbus began to vibrate.

The blonde stewardess was heading back towards the executive seats at the front of the plane. As she opened the curtain dividing the two compartments, one of her colleagues whispered something in her ear. Milos tensed. But the women were laughing. Sharing a rude joke, maybe, or planning what to do during their stopover. The second stewardess had dark hair; otherwise they might have been twins. But Milos wasn't interested in them. He was interested in the way the blonde hadn't closed the curtain properly.

The gap she'd left gave Milos a clear line of sight to the man he was planning to kill.

1

March 1st
09:48
Heathrow Airport, Terminal Two

AN AIRCRAFT roared overhead, invisible in the mist. Even the huge terminal building was just a ghost. People moved like shadows through the gloom.

'747,' said Charlie.

'Yeah, right,' said Alex Chappell. She looked up from the clipboard on her lap. 'Like you can tell.'

'Or a Sopwith Camel. They're easily confused.'

'Charlie Paddon, sometimes you're full of crap.'

'But loveable with it.'

'That's debatable. D'you want to make a move yet?'

'No, let's sit and glower at the frequent fliers a bit longer. They get nervous when they see the police staring at them.'

'You've got an evil streak, Charlie, you know that?'

'Full of crap? Evil streak? It's a wonder you can stand being my partner.'

'I drowned kittens in a former life. You're my punishment.'

Charlie stretched. The red BMW was roomy but he still ended up elbowing the window and catching the brake pedal with his foot. Humming to himself, he adjusted the tilt of the seat. Alex watched with a smile on her face.

'Sometimes I think it's true.'

'What's true?'

'You only joined up because you liked the flash cars.'

He mimed a bullet hit to the heart. 'You got me!'

Charlie had to admit he did like the cars, had done so since before his transfer from the regular Metropolitan Police to the Diplomatic Protection Group. Not because they were flash or fast—Charlie was no boyracer. But somehow they made a difference.

So when, just six months ago, the DPG had taken on selected SO1 functions, it was Charlie who'd led the campaign to keep the iconic red livery. He wouldn't have put it past the bureaucrats to ditch it; after arse-covering, re-branding was their favourite pastime. In the end—and thanks in part to Charlie's lobbying—very little had changed, on the ground at least. There was only one thing he didn't like about the merger: they changed the division's name to Special Operations—Diplomats.

The new name, naturally, boiled down to an unfortunate new acronym.

'It's all right,' said Alex, placing a maternal hand on Charlie's leg. 'I don't mind your obsession with brightly coloured motor vehicles. I know that underneath that tough professional exterior lies the mind of a small child.'

'Are you saying I'm superficial?'

'Only on the surface.'

'All I'm saying is, image counts for something. No, that's not it. Identity, that's the thing. You're a foreign diplomat on your first official visit to London. You need to know immediately who you can trust. That's why I kicked up a fuss about the vehicles.'

'And your point is?'

Charlie gripped the wheel, stared outside. 'I don't know. Maybe my point is that everything matters, all the little details. That's all. It's all important, even the little things. Especially the little things.' He caught his reflection in the glass, saw his frown. He allowed himself a chuckle. 'You know, you haven't put that clipboard down since we got here.'

Alex removed her hand from Charlie's leg and riffled through her papers again. 'Just boning up. It's funny—we don't have a photo of Dunja's translator. What's she called again?'

'Jelenka Levnicki. I know—I didn't recognise the name, either. I don't think she's been over before. Still, when you're Foreign Minister of Croatia you probably get a whole pool of translators to choose from. Maybe Dunja just picks one to match his tie.'

Alex put down the clipboard. 'Don't forget to steer clear of Cromwell Road on the way back to Whitehall. You know what those roadworks were like earlier.'

'Well, Dunja's not due at Whitehall until 11:30. We've got plenty of time.'

All the same, Charlie checked his watch.

He looked out into the fog again. He'd parked the BMW in one of the reserved spaces opposite Terminal Two's weather-worn frontage. Passengers streamed past, hauling luggage; taxis loaded and unloaded; baggage trains slipped like eels through the chaos. It was a scene he'd observed a hundred times, but today the grey mist made everything look strangely alien.

Charlie shivered, suddenly uneasy.

'We should get to work,' he said.

'Right.' Alex made a fist. Alex did the same. They nudged knuckles.

'Keep your knickers clean,' said Charlie.

'Inside and out.'

Charlie unlocked the door, swung it open.

The BMW's built-in printer chattered to life.

Charlie pulled the door shut and reached under the dashboard. As soon as the paper's leading edge popped clear of the printer slot, Charlie grabbed it. He pulled the paper taut, coaxing it out.

'You won't make it go any faster,' said Alex.

Charlie didn't care. He'd seen the page header. It was a memo from Chief Superintendent Brian Burfield. Burfield was a busy man, far too busy to be writing memos to a couple of grunts out in the field.

Something was wrong.

Charlie tried to read the memo as it emerged. Of course, the geeks who installed this kit had fitted the printer so the paper came out upside down. Where was Q when you needed him?

'Well?' said Alex when the printer finally stopped.

Charlie snatched the printout, turned it the right way up.

The following constitutes a Level One security warning. MI6 believes an attempt may be made on Hazbi Dunja's life following his arrival in the UK. Latest intelligence suggests Serbian assassin Javor Milos (see attached) and unknown accomplices may have entered the country under false passports...

Charlie glanced down the page to the profile on Milos.

The grainy mugshot could have been any man born east of the Adriatic.

'Problems?' asked Alex.

'Looks like Dunja's not everyone's flavour of the month,' said Charlie. 'Uh, we're to keep an eye out for one Javor Milos. Thirty-two years old, black hair, beard— there's a picture. Linked to a number of assassination attempts on former Yugoslavian officials over recent years.'

'That's helpful,' said Alex. She peered at the photo. 'He looks like a tough cookie.'

Charlie nodded. 'Maybe his mother loves him. Looks like our day just got more complicated.'

Charlie eyeballed the crowd. Was there an assassin out there? A taxi pulled up nearby, disgorged a trio of women in smart suits. By the time the taxi drove away, the women had already vanished into the fog.

Charlie realised he couldn't see the terminal building any more.

'Fog's getting thicker,' said Alex, echoing his thoughts.

'You're telling me. And you know what? I haven't heard a plane coming in for at least five minutes. I'm beginning to think our visiting VIP might not even reach Britain today.'

'Given the contents of this memo,' said Alex, 'it might be better for Hazbi Dunja if his plane just turned round and flew straight back to Croatia.'

2

March 1st
10:03
Croatia Airlines, Flight OU 312

LIKE Milos, Hazbi Dunja was sitting in an aisle seat.
Beside Dunja, next to the window, sat a woman. Milos
wondered who she was—not a bodyguard, otherwise
their positions would have been reversed. Anyway, Dunja
always boasted that, as a former soldier, he didn't need
security. Milos wondered if he'd still be thinking that in
a few hours' time. The woman must be Dunja's latest
protégé, he guessed, some diplomatic lackey—probably
an assistant—sleeping her way to the top.

Only the back of Dunja's head was visible, but it was
enough to arouse the old anger in Milos. Dunja's hair was
thin, combed over in a vain attempt to hide the growing
bald patch. *Typical of the deceitful bastard,* Milos
thought. *Even tries to deceive himself when he looks in
the mirror.*

For a second or two Milos was back in Zrmanjagrad.
The whine of the Airbus's engines became the rumble of
M84 tank tracks on the deserted streets. He closed his

eyes, heard the crunch of Croat boots on the gravel outside the house, the eerie sound of enemy soldiers shouting into silence. The soldiers were there to 'cleanse' the
town. Only the whole town was deserted. Except for one
house. The house where Milos and his family lived.

The boots came closer, then stopped. Somebody kicked
the door in.

Milos opened his eyes. Before he knew what he was
doing, he'd latched the drop-down tray against the seat
in front and stood up. Now he was walking up the aisle,
towards the executive seats. Towards Dunja. Nobody
looked up. Nobody moved. How could they ignore him?
Couldn't they hear the blood thumping in his head?
Couldn't they feel the fury emanating from him? But the
other passengers were oblivious, hypnotised by the
Hollywood movie playing on their tiny screens. Cabin
crews called the passengers sheep; Milos could see why.

He slipped through the curtain just as the dark-haired
stewardess turned to close it.

'Have I got time before we land?' said Milos, indicating the door to the executive toilet. His head felt clear
again. The anger had faded. The stewardess flashed him
the same fake smile her colleague had used. The smiles
probably came with the uniforms.

'As long as you're quick, sir.'

The toilet was positioned directly opposite the seat occupied by Dunja. It was also engaged, which was exactly
why Milos had asked to use it. Now he had the perfect excuse to loiter in the aisle, barely a metre from his target.

Dunja was leafing through the pages of *Croatia,* the
in-flight magazine. He seemed unaware of Milos's presence. Absently, he pulled a tissue from his pocket, blew
his nose. His eyes looked tired, rimmed with red.

Hazbi Dunja had a cold.

I could just reach out, Milos thought. *Reach out, put my hands to your throat and squeeze the life from you.*

Milos felt his fingers tingle. But he didn't allow them to move.

Besides, after what Dunja had done, the bastard didn't deserve a quick, clean death, nor a public one. This was a private affair. He would die slowly, in agony, away from the world.

Hazbi Dunja had found an article in the magazine that interested him. He flattened the magazine with his right hand, the hand that was famously missing the last joint of its index finger.

'Taken off by a Serbian bullet during the siege of Dubrovnik,' was the story Dunja usually told the press. The media loved printing pictures of Dunja waving with his deformed hand. It made him look like a war hero. Milos was the only man in the world who knew how Dunja had really lost the end of his finger.

'Excuse me, sir,' said a woman's voice in Milos's ear, 'but I'm going to have to ask you to return to the economy seats.'

Milos swung round, fists curling. The blonde stewardess met his glare with her paper-thin smile. He saw himself take that smile and smear it into a bloody mess. Saw himself snap her neck and toss her like a doll to the floor...

One by one, his muscles unbunched.

'I'm waiting for the toilet,' muttered Milos under his breath. He didn't want to make a scene. Even though he'd shaved off his beard, he couldn't risk Dunja recognising him. Not yet.

'The economy class toilets are back that way, sir.'

'I'm sorry,' he said. 'All the toilets back there were engaged. I knew we were landing soon, so I didn't want to
leave it too late.'

'I understand, sir,' said the blonde. Her voice was hard
and glassy. 'But I see the economy toilets have become
vacant while you've been waiting here. And this one is
still engaged.' She paused. 'So, if you'd care to make your
way back to your section of the plane?'

'Yes,' said Milos. 'Of course.'

He turned to go. To his relief, Dunja was still absorbed
in the magazine. But the woman at his side was staring
straight at Milos.

Their eyes met only briefly before the woman looked
away. Milos carried a snapshot of her all the way back
down the aisle. *A dancer,* he thought. Even sitting in the
stiff Airbus seat, the woman had seemed somehow
poised. There was a kind of strength in her face, a mus-
cular quality to her body.

Her dark eyes had danced over his.

I'll bet you make her earn her promotions, Hazbi Dunja.

Milos decided he'd take the woman, as well. He'd
make her watch while he dealt with Dunja. By the time
Milos had finished, she'd be bending over backwards to
please him. Literally.

Everything now depended on Anton and his team. By
now they'd be deployed in the terminal building at
Heathrow, preparing to distract the security services.
Anton would have positioned a suspicious-looking holdall behind a column at the north-east end of the terminal.
The minute Flight OU 312 landed, he'd make an anonymous call to the airport police. Just as Hazbi Dunja and
his athletic translator left customs, they'd find themselves
caught up in a full-blown security alert.

At first Milos had been doubtful about the plan. He preferred to keep things low-key. But Anton had persuaded him.

'Since 9/11, everything's on a hair-trigger,' he'd said. 'You shout "jump", everyone hits the ceiling. Plus, you know how it goes. They'll assume they're looking for Islamic extremists. A few grubby Serbs should be able to slip right through their net.'

Milos had warmed to the idea. The positioning of Anton's fake bomb meant any in-bound passengers already cleared through immigration would be evacuated through the main entrance. Dunja would be among them. There'd be crowds, jostling. There'd be a bottle-neck at the doors.

The bottle-neck would give Milos time to catch up with Dunja. The confusion would allow him to hustle Dunja into the car Anton would have waiting, leaving the police to scratch their heads over a large leather holdall containing four beach towels and a pornographic magazine.

The British government would have arranged an escort for the visiting Foreign Minister. But right now the security services were more interested in the Middle East than Eastern Europe. They wouldn't be expecting trouble. They'd send a couple of fresh-faced officers with pop-guns, just to show willing. These officers, too, would be caught up in the confusion.

So confident was Anton that the plan would work, he'd even suggested they scrap the idea of tailing Dunja on to the plane.

'Nothing's going to happen until Dunja lands at Heathrow,' he'd said. 'Why risk being spotted just so you can watch him dozing in his seat?'

On that point they'd argued. Milos had won. Anton

had orchestrated the mission, but Milos was the conductor. His word was final.

'I go on the aircraft with Dunja,' he'd said. 'This discussion is over.'

Anton couldn't understand that Milos wasn't just an assassin tailing his target: he was a predator stalking his prey. Over the years, anticipation had become a drug for Milos. He sometimes wondered what he'd do when Dunja was dead and it was all, finally, over.

That was the difference between them. To Anton it was just another operation.

To Milos it was everything.

There was a chime above Milos's head. He glanced up: the FASTEN SEATBELT light had come on. Outside, cloud had enveloped the Airbus completely.

Another chime, this one from the PA system. The pilot, getting ready to calm the sheep before bringing them into the fold.

'Ladies and gentleman, this is Captain Bakalar. I'm afraid the fog over London has thickened considerably since we took off this morning. Unfortunately, Heathrow is cutting back air traffic, which means we must divert to Stansted Airport, where weather conditions are a little better. If you have any concerns about your onward journey within the United Kingdom, please speak to a member of our cabin crew, who will be able to advise…'

Milos tensed in his seat and ignored the remainder of the announcement. His fingers closed on the arm of his seat, gripping hard. The veins on the back of his hand bulged. The man beside him stared. Milos uncurled his fingers, one by one. He smiled at the man.

'I really hate the landings,' he said, 'don't you?'

The man smiled back, reassured.

Milos pretended to relax. But his mind was racing. So much for Anton's assertion they didn't need to follow Dunja on to the plane! Now it was all up to Milos. By the time Anton realised what was happening—and found out which airport they'd been diverted to—Hazbi Dunja would be down and in the clear.

Unless Milos could get to him first.

Milos continued to smile. It seemed poetic, somehow, that it came down to just the two of them, as it had been just the two of them, in the end, in that house in Zrmanjagrad, all those years ago. Still, it would be a hell of a challenge.

Like the pilot easing Flight OU 312 through the fog on to its new approach path, Javor Milos was now flying blind.

3

'BLOODY phone,' said Henry Worthington, glaring at the offending device. 'Why do you never ring when I want you to?'

The phone sat, stubborn and silent, on Henry's gleaming walnut desk. Beside it, Henry's laptop was still frozen halfway through the act of rebooting. Henry yanked the power cable loose, stuffed it back in again, hit the restart button. The laptop winked an LED and started its inscrutable electronic chuckling again. *If the damn thing doesn't reboot this time*, Henry decided, *it's going through the window*.

Henry turned his attention back to the document he'd managed to print off before the computer locked up. There was something reassuring about black ink on a white page: you knew where you stood with a piece of paper.

'Bring back the typing pool,' he muttered.

Actually, Henry Worthington wasn't the technophobe he'd have everyone believe. Encrypted email, for instance, had been a godsend to the intelligence community. It meant Henry didn't have to share his thoughts with anyone he didn't want to. And while he wasn't a spook himself, Henry dealt with enough of them to have developed a healthy respect for the phrase, 'need to know'.

As secretary to the Security and Intelligence Coordinator, Henry saw himself as a kind of air traffic controller. On any one day he had a lot of people feeding him conflicting information, and making conflicting demands. All of them trying to steer a different course. It was his job to make sure it was safe landings all round.

Of course, everyone had a different idea about what that meant. As far as Henry was concerned, a safe landing meant any outcome that damaged neither the Cabinet Office nor Her Majesty's Government.

Nor, most important of all, Henry Worthington.

While the laptop whirred, he picked up the printout. Hazbi Dunja's itinerary. It was typical of the kind of paperwork he had to shuffle. The Croatian Foreign Minister needed nurse-maiding through the usual round of meetings, photo opportunities and back-scratching bun fights.

A handshake with the British Foreign Secretary, followed by a working lunch with a group of Croatian ex-pats eager to raise the profile of their immigrant support scheme…and so on. By evening, a red-eyed Dunja would be on board another plane on his way to Edinburgh where, tomorrow, he was due to address the Scottish Assembly.

Henry's role in all this was both to oil the wheels and make sure they didn't fall off. Dunja's arrival at Heathrow in (he checked the carriage clock on the marble mantelpiece) ten minutes' time was the first of many safe landings he needed to engineer over the coming days. He wasn't anticipating any problems, certainly not today, the schedule for which looked as routine as they came. Tomorrow might be different, though.

It was this Scottish Assembly business that bothered Henry. Dunja wore the skin of a diplomat, but underneath he was still the freedom fighter he'd always been. So, for the Scottish Executive to invite him to deliver a speech on—of all things—nationhood was, in Henry's opinion, asking for trouble.

The previous winter had seen some lively debate in the Scottish Parliament on the thorny old issues of sovereignty, devolution and the independent Scottish nation. It was ever thus, of course. Just one more reason Hadrian had built the wall. These days, debate took place in the civilised Miralles-designed halls at Holyrood, but it was no less heated for that.

Bringing in Hazbi Dunja—a former soldier who had taken up arms to lead his country to independence—would certainly stoke the fires. He only had to wave to show off his war wounds: that trademark missing finger. He might as well strip naked, paint himself blue and run into Holyrood screaming at the top of his voice.

The man will come, Henry reassured himself, *and he will go. Safe landings—that's all that counts.*

The phone rang. Relieved, Henry lifted the receiver.

'Worthington,' he said.

'Morning, Henry. Glad I caught you. Thought I'd give you a quick buzz to see if Dunja's turned up yet. The Heathrow webcams are looking a bit murky. Any idea what's going on?'

Henry suppressed a groan. If there was anyone guaranteed to give him a migraine it was Jack McClintock.

'Hello, Jack,' he said. 'I'm afraid I can't comment on that one.'

'Come on, Henry, you always say that. You know I always get something out of you in the end, so why not save us both the effort and give me a scoop?'

'There is no scoop, Jack. So why don't *you* save yourself the effort and hang up?'

'Not in my nature. Like a terrier, me. You know they call me Jack Russell? Look, Henry, how about this: I'll tell you what I do know about Dunja's visit, and you grunt once for true and twice for false. What do you say?'

Henry smiled, despite himself. Jack was the most persistent reporter he knew. And the most annoying. On the other hand, it suited Henry to have a tame hack through whom—from time to time—he could leak information.

The situation was only marginally complicated by the fact that Jack McClintock was Henry's brother-in-law.

'I still say,' replied Henry, 'that I have no comment to make at this time.'

'Well, then,' said Jack, 'just humour me a minute. I've been doing some digging. Seems to me Hazbi Dunja's past is even murkier than those airport webcams. You know how Dunja always skirts round the subject of ethnic cleansing? Claims he was an honourable soldier, never supported the use of torture for military ends?'

'He has always made his position on the issue very clear.'

'Right. Well, it's just that, when you look at some of the places he says he was during the war, and the dates he says he was there…well, it's hard to believe he didn't at least witness some of the atrocities. Take Operation Thunder, for instance…'

'This is all very interesting, Jack, but I'm expecting an important call…'

'More important than mine?'

'When I gave you my direct line number, Jack, I asked you to treat it with respect. Now please, I've got a lot to get through this morning.'

'Okay, Henry, you win. And don't get me wrong, I appreciate you letting me use the bat-phone.'

'I'll speak to you later, Jack. When we've got something to talk about.'

'You could just give me a quote now? Embargo it if you like. I won't blab. You know me.'

'Yes, Jack, I do. Goodbye.'

'Okay. Say hi to Mary. Tell her my freezer's empty, if she wants to send round another one of her casseroles. Oh, and remind her it's Derek's birthday on Friday.'

Henry put down the phone. It rang again instantly. He snatched it up.

'Worthington.'

'Henry, it's Brian.'

At last, Henry thought.

'Good morning, Brian. I trust the welcome mat is out for our visitor?'

'Well, I've got news for you, if that's what you mean.'

It occurred to Henry that, whether he was delivering good news or bad, Brian Burfield always sounded miserable. 'That is what I mean, Brian. Has Dunja landed?'

'No. The plane's been diverted to Stansted. Heathrow's fogbound. Wouldn't you know it?'

Henry glared at the itinerary, resisting the urge to screw it up and hurl it across the room. There went the schedule! He'd have to call the Foreign Secretary's office, try to re-schedule the meeting for later in the day. They were probably still good for lunch with the Croats…

'I trust you've got the situation in hand, Brian,' he said. He grabbed a pen, started scribbling in the margin.

Now he thought of it, Dunja had a forty-five minute slot before he was due to get on the Edinburgh plane. Maybe they could fit the Foreign Secretary in then.

'Don't worry,' said Brian. 'I've got two officers on their way to Stansted right now. Paddon and Chappell. They're good. Fog might slow them down, but I've briefed the Stansted police. They'll keep Dunja plied with tea and biscuits until my people arrive.'

Brian seemed about to say more, then checked himself.

'Is there anything else, Brian?' said Henry.

The briefest pause. 'No. You heard from Nick Luard today?'

'I make a point of never speaking to MI6 before lunch. Any reason I should?'

'No. No reason.'

Henry waited to see if Brian would say any more. He didn't. 'You'll keep me informed as the situation develops, won't you, Brian?'

'Of course.'

Henry's attention had wandered back to the itinerary. What if this messed up the schedule so much they couldn't get Dunja on the Edinburgh plane tonight? Things were sticky enough in Scotland as it was.

'How are things at Holyrood, by the way?' he said. 'I gather your people were late arranging the security checks.'

'It's fine,' said Brian. He sounded defensive. 'The mix-up was at their end, not ours. I sent Alex Chappell up there yesterday—those Celtic clowns made her hang around half the morning before finally letting her do her thing. But everything looks clear. Once Alex has helped Paddon deliver Dunja to the City, she'll be heading back up there again to keep an eye on things.'

'Is that everything?'

'Pretty much. We were worried about a group of travellers who've set up camp on the south side of Holyrood Park. Local police did the usual soft handshake; they seem a reasonable bunch, say they're only stopping a few more nights. Not worth making headlines just to move them on.'

'All right, Brian. Tell your people to get to Stansted as fast as they can. We've got a lot to get through today. Let me know as soon as you've got Dunja under your wing.'

'You'll be the first to know, Henry.'

Henry put down the phone. Things weren't as bad as he'd first thought. Still, he was going to have to do some juggling. The worst part was the short notice. There was nothing he hated more than making apologetic phone calls to other civil servants even more protective of their arses than he was.

The laptop had booted up at last. The screensaver had activated while Henry had been on the phone; psychedelic patterns splashed across the screen. He nudged the touchpad and the screensaver vanished, revealing familiar icons lined up on his desktop picture: a beach in Madeira.

No fog in Madeira, he thought bitterly.

He spent a few more minutes scribbling notes. Then he picked up the phone and made the first difficult call of the day, unaware of quite how difficult the subsequent calls were going to be.

4

March 1st
10:46
Stansted Airport

THE SKY over Stansted was clear. It was hard to believe
Heathrow was crippled by fog. Milos sat impatiently, waiting for the Airbus to taxi up to the covered gantry. But the
plane stopped short; minutes later a mobile staircase rolled
up to the forward doors. Behind the stairs was a train of
shuttle buses ready to take the passengers to the terminal.

There followed an agonising wait as the first-class passengers disembarked. Two stewardesses—one of them
Milos's blonde nemesis—loitered in the aisle between
the two cabins like smiling security guards, making sure
the proles didn't get ideas above their station.

At last it was Milos's turn. He edged forward with the
rest of the economy class passengers. When he stepped
out on to the stairs, the full extent of the chaos became
apparent. The aprons and taxiways were littered with aircraft; some almost touched wingtips as they jockeyed to
find space to unload. He didn't envy the ground staff
having to deal with this lot.

The first bus was pulling away. Milos was dismayed—
though hardly surprised—to see Dunja and the translator inside. He hurried down the steps and made sure he
was on bus number two.

Immigration looked like a refugee camp. All the routes
had been opened up, but still the place was packed wall-
to-wall. Milos went for what looked like the shortest
queue. And there was Dunja, just twenty metres in front
of him, his balding head a tantalising target. Milos tried
to shoulder his way forwards through a group of young
men speaking French. They locked arms and swore at
him, refusing to let him through. He fell back. He
couldn't afford to draw attention to himself. If security
picked him up, the mission was over.

Slowly the queue shuffled forward. Despite the scrum,
the customs officials were being as diligent as ever.
Tempers began to fray. When a young official closed one
of the customs gates, forcing a whole line of passengers
to file into another queue, a scuffle broke out. Airport security pounced on the perpetrators, to the amusement of
the Frenchmen. Milos took the opportunity to slip past.

All the while he kept his eyes on Dunja. His only option was to stay close. He was carrying no weapons—not
that he needed a weapon to kill. But this wasn't the time
or place. With luck, Anton was already on his way here.
By the time he cleared customs, Milos's team would be
back together. Then he could go to work.

Dunja's diplomatic papers got him through without incident. As Milos presented his false EU passport, he held
his breath. The customs official flipped the passport open,
looked from the photo to Milos and back again. Milos held
the man's gaze. The official tilted the photo into the light,
peered closer. Milos wanted to snatch the passport and run.

The official snapped the passport shut and handed it back.

'Thank you, sir,' he said. 'Next.'

Milos hurried through the gate, fighting to control his pace.

When he reached the main concourse he stopped, dazzled by the sunlight pouring through the glass ceiling. He looked out across a sea of faces; there was a roar like the sea, the sound of a stadium crowd. How would he ever find them?

White columns branched out to support the roof. They were plastered with technology: information screens, electronic departure boards. Milos ran to a discarded luggage trolley and stood on it to peer into the crowd, seeking out his quarry. On the far wall he spotted a door marked AIRPORT SECURITY. Had Dunja presented himself to the authorities?

Then he looked towards the big doors at the end of the concourse, and saw him.

Hazbi Dunja and the female translator were in the middle of a crush of people forcing their way out on to the road. There was no mistaking the man: the comb-over gave him away every time.

Jumping off the column, Milos bulldozed through the crowd. When people got in his way, he used boots, elbows and harsh language to clear a path. Now he was clear of customs, he didn't care about making a scene. The window of opportunity was closing fast.

Miraculously, as he reached the doors, the crowd thinned. He burst outside, and there was Dunja, right in front him. Only he was already in the back seat of a taxi, the passenger door was slamming shut, and the driver was turning the wheel and pulling out into the traffic. Next to

Dunja sat the woman. She was leaning close, almost intimately so, whispering something in his ear.

As the taxi accelerated away, Milos ran out into the road, ignoring the honking horns and shouts of abuse. For a second he considered running after them. But they were already too far away.

A minibus was trying to pull into the slot left by the taxi. The driver leaned out of his window and yelled at Milos to get out of the way. Milos stepped back on to the kerb, but not before treating the driver to a traditional Serbian hand gesture.

Passengers continued to pour out of the terminal building. Milos stood firm, resisting the tide. Reaching inside his jacket, he pulled out his mobile and dialled the first number in the memory. After two rings, he heard a familiar voice say, 'Milos?'

'Anton. I'm at Stansted Airport. Where are you?'

'Coming your way. We heard about the diversion. But the traffic is very bad. We'll be at least half an hour.'

'Not quick enough. Just do your best. Call me when you get here. I'll tell you what's going on then.'

In the distance, the sign on the roof of the taxi was just visible above the rest of the cars. In another minute it would be out of sight and all hope of catching Hazbi Dunja would be lost. He thrust the phone back inside his jacket and took a deep breath.

He was on his own.

5

March 1st
10:58
M11, Bishop's Stortford

EVERY lane was jammed solid. Charlie lit the blues and swerved on to the hard shoulder, taking the exit ramp at seventy. Reaching the roundabout at the top, he ploughed a furrow through the traffic, overtook a dawdling Citroën, and arrowed the BMW north-east towards Stansted Airport.

Alex was on the radio, talking to the Stansted Airport police.

'Yes,' she was saying, 'I'm sure you're busy with all the extra passengers…yes, it must be chaos…'

She kept trying to speak, kept biting her lip as the policeman on the other end interrupted her. He was doing a good job of winding her up. Given her natural calm, Charlie thought, that was quite an achievement.

'I understand all that,' Alex said, 'but you've got to appreciate our position. Our VIP will be with you shortly—if he isn't already—and it's imperative he gets a proper escort…yes, yes, I know that's our job. We just need you to take care of him until we get there. We're only a few minutes away now…yes, his name is Hazbi Dunja. He's…no, Dunja. D-U-N…'

So it went on. It didn't matter that Charlie couldn't hear the other end of the conversation. The tone of Alex's voice told him everything he needed to know.

Within sight of Stansted they hit an even worse jam. The cars ahead pulled in to the side of the road, but up ahead an articulated lorry was just too large an obstruction. Confusion in the air had caused gridlock on the ground. Charlie punched the steering wheel in frustration.

'There must be a quicker way!'

'Roger,' said Alex. She'd finished trying to communicate with the chimps at Stansted, and examined the map on her knees. 'If you can reverse back a hundred yards, there's a farm track on the left that meets a service road.' Charlie wound down the window and waved at the cars behind, before completing a five-point turn. The other drivers stared like dumb cattle as he drove the wrong way back along the road. With the hedgerow whipping against the side of the vehicle, he brought the car to a pair of farm gates, thankfully open and hanging off their hinges. He steered the BMW between the posts and gunned the accelerator up a metalled track towards some low sheds. A cattle grid rattled beneath the wheels.

'Go right,' said Alex. A passage opened up between two sheds. Charlie dodged into it. 'Left again at the end should bring us on to the airport road.'

Better than sat-nav, thought Charlie, as he worked the car through the labyrinth of service roads.

Even so, the journey had taken too long. Charlie was getting twitchy.

At last they reached the terminal. Charlie clipped the

kerb, slammed on the brakes, was out of the door almost before the BMW had stopped moving. There were vehicles everywhere. Two taxis had collided and the drivers were arguing over the damage.

It wasn't much better inside. The arrivals lobby was in uproar. There were queues at every counter as diverted travellers tried to arrange transfer flights, hire cars, book taxis. His ears were battered by the sound of several thousand people all trying to shout at once.

'Where's our contact?' he said to Alex.

'He said he'd meet us at customs,' she said, pointing.

They strode through the crowd, parting the waves. Most people stood back; a few grumbled. Twice Charlie cracked his shin on a wayward suitcase, mumbling apologies.

'Plane's in,' said Alex, spotting an arrivals board.

Charlie followed her gaze, scanned the list. There it was: *Croatia Airlines, Flight OU 312.*

Hazbi Dunja was in the country.

A tall, pale police sergeant was waiting for them near the customs exit, shoulders slumped, sleeves rolled to the elbow. He looked like he'd done a week of night shifts. When he saw Charlie, he straightened up. But he didn't smile. Charlie's sense of unease deepened.

'Mike Wallace,' said the sergeant, shaking both their hands. 'Glad you're here.'

'What's the news?' said Charlie, pitching his voice for just the three of them. 'Where have you put our man?'

'That's just it,' said Wallace. 'I'm sorry to say, Elvis has left the building.'

The trip from Heathrow had pumped Charlie full of adrenaline. This hit him like a punch to the gut. 'Tell us what happened,' said Alex, calming Charlie with a touch to his wrist.

'We clocked them quickly enough,' said Wallace. 'Managed to monitor their progress while they proceeded through immigration. But, well, there were six flights disembarking at exactly the same time, four of them diverted from Heathrow. Believe me, we were faced with a very big bunch of unhappy bunnies. There was a lot more to think about than a couple of wandering Serbs.'

'Croatians,' said Charlie.

'Is that where you lost them?' asked Alex. 'In immigration?'

'Yes. And I know what you're thinking—I mean, the two of them were easy enough to spot. Him with that ridiculous comb-over and his—what is she, a translator?—well, she cuts a keen figure, as my old man used to say. The problem was they seemed to be in a right old hurry to get through customs. And, like I said, the place was heaving. We just lost them in the crowd. When we finally picked them up again they were already out through the main doors and into a minicab.'

That brought Charlie up short. 'A *minicab*?' he said.

Wallace nodded. 'I know. Doesn't add up, does it? I mean, they must have been expecting to be met, despite the diversion from Heathrow. You'd have thought they'd have made themselves known to us. Instead they just barrelled right through customs like their tails were on fire.'

'All the same,' said Alex, 'it's a pity you let them get away.'

She could go from cool to icy in a blink. Charlie had suffered his share of Alex Chappell frostbite over the years, and felt some sympathy as Wallace squirmed.

'All I can say is we did our best,' said Wallace. 'Things were no better out on the road than they were in here. We had two officers right behind your VIPs as they went out the doors and then all hell broke loose. Some despatch rider ran right up to our men and started shouting about how someone had nicked his bike. His nose was bleeding—he was making one hell of a scene. This group of women started panicking—I don't know, thought it was a terrorist attack or something. By the time the officers had calmed things down, the VIPs were nowhere in sight. Then one of them spotted the bloke—what's his name, Gunja?—just as the minicab accelerated away.'

'Shit,' said Charlie. 'We must have missed them by minutes.'

Sergeant Wallace swept his hands back through his hair. The sunlight flooding through the roof lights made him look paler than ever. Except for the dark circles under his eyes. 'Look, for what it's worth, I'm sorry. But you can see what we're up against here. If there's anything more we can do…'

Charlie looked out across the sea of anxious faces. Passengers were shouting at desk clerks, into mobile phones, at each other.

'Actually,' he said, 'there is.'

Five minutes later, he was standing in a long, dark room facing a bank of thirty-two flat-screen monitors. Each monitor showed different views of the airport complex: check-ins, lounges, baggage reclaim areas, service roads, taxi stands…

In the office next door, Alex was putting a call in to Brian Burfield. She had some bad news to break. The glass between the office and the CCTV room was tinted; Alex was just a silhouette against a distant window. Charlie watched her as she spoke to their boss. From the way she was moving her hands, he knew it wasn't going down well.

He left her to it, turned his attention to the computer screens.

'No,' Sergeant Wallace was saying to the man hunched over the operating desk, 'just the exterior cameras.'

The man's fingers rattled over his keyboard. He took a swig from the Pepsi can on the desk and hit Return. Three monitors showed the road outside the terminal. On the left-hand screen, Charlie's BMW was clearly visible.

'Fifteen minutes should do it,' said Wallace.

More key-rattling. The images on the monitors juddered, then the time-code jolted backwards. The BMW vanished; a black cab took its place. People streamed past the cameras, blurred and silvery.

'Can't you get a better picture?' asked Charlie.

'Time of day,' said Wallace. 'Bright sunlight pushes up the contrast and the cameras can't cope. We're due for an upgrade, but you know how it is.'

Charlie leaned closer, peering from one screen to the next, trying to pick out faces in the crowd.

'There!' he said, jabbing his finger against the centre screen.

'Please don't touch the monitor,' said the operator. He grabbed a wet-wipe and fussed over the print Charlie had left. Charlie resisted the urge to up-end his Pepsi all over his prissy head.

It was Hazbi Dunja, no doubt about it. Wallace had been right: that antique hairstyle was a giveaway. Close beside Dunja, practically hugging him in fact, was a broad-shouldered woman in a long coat. They looked like people in a hurry.

That must be Jelenka Levnicki, thought Charlie, *the translator. Looks like she doesn't want to get left behind.*

The operator stabbed keys, switching angles to follow

the two Croatians across the road. As they passed from
the shadow of the terminal, Levnicki flagged down a
passing minicab. Sunlight caught her arm, turning it to
white fire. A van drove past, close, obscuring the view on
all three monitors. Charlie cursed. By the time the van
had driven off, Dunja was already inside the minicab;
Levnicki followed him in without a backward glance.

Now an airport shuttle bus was in the way. Charlie
craned his neck as if he could see round. When the bus
moved away, the minicab was gone.

'Grab the best frames you can of that cab,' said
Charlie. 'I want everything from the tyre pressures to the
driver's inside leg.'

As soon as he'd got the prints, Charlie shouldered
through the door into the office. Alex had just come off
the phone.

'How's Burfield?'

'Philosophical,' said Alex. 'Oh, and furious, too. I kept
it short, then called the local traffic unit. They're standing by. What have we got?'

Together, they pored over the prints. Harsh sunlight
and other vehicles had conspired to obscure any identi-
fying marks on the minicab. They couldn't even work out
what colour the cab was.

'Well,' said Alex, picking up the best print and angling
it towards the window, 'it's a Skoda. I think. Can't make
out the number plate.'

'What about the sign on the roof?' said Charlie.
'There's usually a phone number.'

'Here,' said Alex in triumph. 'Zero, one, two, seven,
nine…looks like…six…one…something. The rest's just
a blur.'

'Good enough.'

Charlie scribbled the partial phone number on the back of one of the prints. Wallace was just coming out of the CCTV room. Charlie gave him the number.

'Get one of your people to trace that,' he said. 'Local cab firm.'

He thumbed through the remaining prints, willing them to give up the information he needed. They refused. He tossed them aside.

'They say a picture speaks a thousand words,' he said, 'but these ones aren't talking.'

'We'll get the cab,' said Alex. 'They won't get away.'

'Every minute we waste here they *are* getting away.' Charlie shook his head. 'Why a minicab, Alex? Why not just wait for us?'

'Maybe they'd got wind this Javor Milos character was looking for them. The Croatians have intelligence too, you know. Maybe they were worried Milos would be waiting for them at the airport and decided to keep on the move.'

Charlie was silent for a moment as he tried this out. There was something missing here, something that mattered.

'The traffic boys will pick them up,' Alex went on, 'once we get the cab's ID. Dunja will probably head straight for Whitehall anyway. You never know, he might even be on time for his first appointment!'

Sergeant Wallace was waving to them across the office. 'We've got the cabbies,' he called. 'I'll patch it through.'

The phone on the next desk rang. Charlie grabbed the receiver.

'This is Officer Paddon,' he said. 'Who am I speaking to, please?'

The woman at the end of the line sounded very young and very cross.

'Bishop Cars. Look, we're real busy right now.'

'I'm sure you are, Miss…?'

'Fox. Leanna Fox.'

'All right, Leanna. I need you to tell me if you've sent any cars to Stansted Airport in the last twenty minutes.'

The operator laughed down the line. 'Have we! Mister, we done nothing *but* send cars to Stansted! Like I says, we're busy.'

'The car we're looking for is a Skoda…'

'Well, that covers about half of 'em!'

'It's a Skoda and it made a pick-up outside the terminal at…' Charlie checked the time-code on the bottom of one of the prints, '…10:54. Does that narrow it down?'

Leanna sighed. In the background, Charlie could hear at least three phones ringing and someone swearing. 'Hold on. I'll check.'

Charlie felt his hand tighten on the receiver as the seconds ticked past. He rolled his eyes at Alex, who infuriated him by standing calm, arms folded, waiting.

Then he heard Leanna say, 'Ere, now that's weird.'

'What?' he said. Now he had the receiver in a death-grip. 'What's weird?'

'Car four-seven. Looks like it's gone off the system.'

Charlie wrote '47' on the nearest print. Eyebrows raised, he waggled it at Alex. She started examining the prints again. 'System?' he said. 'What d'you mean?'

'The satellite wossname,' said Leanna, as if she was explaining it to a toddler. 'Tells us whether the drivers are doing what they're paid to, or parked up in a lay-by eating a full English.'

'You can track all your vehicles?'

'Course we can.'

Alex rammed one of the prints under Charlie's nose. She'd ringed a badge on the Skoda's rear bumper. The numbers on the badge were so blurred they'd missed them first time around. But now they knew what they were looking for...

'That's it,' said Charlie.

'That's what?' asked Leanna.

'Car four-seven. That's the one we're looking for.'

'Well, like I said, it's gone off the system. Satellite must be on the blink. Or the driver's switched it off. I'm sorry, love, you might be looking for it, but you ain't gonna find it.'

Charlie shook his head. What else could go wrong today?

'Can you at least tell me its last position?' he said. 'Where was it just before the tracking system went down?'

Somewhere south of here, with any luck, heading straight for the City of London.

Another sigh. 'Wait a minute...here we go...'

Charlie listened. Heart sinking, he wrote down exactly what Leanna told him. Finally he asked her for the car's registration and the name of the driver. Even before he'd finished, Alex was on the radio. As Charlie wrote, she relayed the information to the traffic police. They both came off their respective lines at the same instant. Exchanging nothing but a glance, each knowing exactly what the other was thinking, they ran across the office to the fire escape, the quickest way back down to the road. They descended the stairs two at a time.

'How's your maths?' asked Charlie, as they burst through the doors at the bottom. 'Because this isn't adding up for me.'

'Me, neither,' said Alex. 'But don't worry—we'll catch them.'

They reached the BMW, jumped inside.

'Quickest way out of here?' said Charlie, gunning the engine.

'Left at the end,' said Alex. 'There's a service road.'

The BMW skidded out of Stansted.

Heading north.

6

March 1st
11:33
A1 Northbound

JAVOR Milos couldn't feel his hands.

When he'd ridden the stolen motorbike out of Stansted the sun had been shining. After just twenty kilometres the mist had descended again. The temperature had plummeted and the wind-chill was ferocious. What a godforsaken country!

He wished he'd thought to grab the despatch rider's gloves.

The despatch rider had turned up just as the taxi disappeared behind the terminal building. Milos knew instinctively that this was it: his only chance. The rider pulled up to the kerb just a few metres away, took off his helmet and started checking his paperwork. He looked flustered, in a hurry.

Even before he'd left the saddle, Milos was striding towards him.

He grabbed the courier's helmet in one hand, his shoulder in the other. The badge on the rider's lapel said DAVE.

He shoved Dave backwards but kept his grip on the helmet. Dave sat down, hard on the ground. He was up faster than Milos would have liked, shouting obscenities and bunching his fist. But Milos was already astride the bike, pulling on the helmet. Dave seized his assailant's arm and got an elbow in the ribs for his pains. As he came back for more, Milos punched him on the nose. Blood pouring down his face, Dave reeled back, shouting for the police. By the time they came, Milos was gone.

He'd caught up with the taxi readily enough: there was only one way out of the airport complex. Since then he'd just sat on its tail. Dunja knew he was being chased, Milos was sure of that. Otherwise why would he run? But it seemed that he, too, was content to play a waiting game.

That was fine by Milos. He had no actual plan; he just knew he wasn't letting Dunja out of his sight. He knew he should be angry. Despite all the careful preparations— the nights he and Anton had spent poring over flight schedules and airport schematics—it had come to this: a headlong chase across the English countryside. It should have felt like a disaster.

So why does it feel like fate?

Now, nearly a hundred kilometres up the road, he was even beginning to experience a perverse kind of pleasure.

A silver-grey Ford pulled out in front of Milos. He kicked down a gear, accelerated past. The Honda responded with a smooth rumble. The man behind the wheel of the Ford looked like a sales rep: chinless, soft-skinned. He watched the bike with an envious look. A cheap jacket swung in the back window. Milos raised one frozen hand in a mock salute and swung back into the middle lane.

The bike he'd stolen was a real beauty: a Honda 250,

with a bright yellow fuel tank and sleek panniers on the back. Fast and lean, if a little conspicuous. Perfect for keeping up with a runaway taxi. Useless for bringing it to a standstill.

Milos had grown up with motorbikes, had loved to ride his father's old NSU Fox round the paddock in Zrmanjagrad. The NSU's throaty exhaust note had been part of the soundtrack of his childhood. That, and the cough of the crows in the pines behind the house.

Something made him look left. He was passing a stand of weathered oaks. An explosion of crows burst from the upper branches, a dark cloud in the grey sky.

A shiver ran up his spine. He adjusted his grip on the throttle and leaned into the wind.

The road was curving slowly north-east. Through breaks in the patchy mist, he saw grey fields, distant chimneys. Flat, dull countryside, not a decent hill in sight, let alone a mountain. A signpost told him the next town was Huntingdon. How long would he be stuck in this saddle?

However long it takes, he thought.

The kilometres fell behind him. His mind started to wander. Instead of the Honda's engine he seemed to hear hoofbeats. He was a warrior prince, racing to battle...

In his inside pocket, his mobile started vibrating.

Immediately, Milos cut across to the inside lane. He dropped his speed as much as he dared, took one hand off the grips and opened his jacket. The wind smashed against his ribs. The zip snagged his knuckle, drawing blood. He didn't feel a thing.

He pulled out the mobile. The number on the display was Luka's, Anton's cousin and one of their best hunts-men. Right now he would be sitting in the passenger seat of a silver Jaguar with Anton at the wheel. With luck they'd be somewhere near Stansted. Awaiting instructions.

With a thumb that seemed to belong to someone else, Milos took the call.

Even with the visor back and the mobile jammed into his helmet, he couldn't hear a word Luka was saying. It didn't matter. Luka knew when to stop talking and listen.

'I'm heading north on the A1,' Milos yelled. 'Near a town called Huntingdon. I'm on a yellow motorbike. Shit—wait a second!'

Although he'd slowed, he was coming up fast on another vehicle: a Renault, dawdling in the inside lane. The man driving it was wearing a flat cap and looked about two hundred years old. Milos dropped his hand—still holding the mobile—to the handlebars and nudged the bike round. As he crossed the white line, a second car flashed past in the middle lane, honking madly. The nearside wing mirror missed him by centimetres. He corrected his drift. The lane ahead was clear but Dunja's minicab was just a blue spot, almost out of sight.

'I can't talk for long!' he shouted into the mobile. 'Get on my tail. Catch me up. Tell Anton break the speed limit but don't get caught. Dunja's in a blue taxi. I'm keeping as close as I dare. When you see me, you'll see the taxi. Shadow me. When there's a service station, go past. Use the unmarked police car routine. Put the blue light on the dashboard. Force them over. Then we'll take them! Text me back, let me know you got all that.'

With his disembodied thumb, he ended the call.

He spent the next minute making up the ground he'd lost. Huntingdon slipped past on his right; the mist made it look like a child's sketch of a town. He prayed Dunja hadn't left the motorway while he'd been talking to Anton.

As he flew under a bridge, the mobile buzzed again, just once. This time he didn't bother to slow down, just pulled out the phone. On the screen was a little envelope icon. He opened the message, which read:

UNDERSTOOD—L

Milos stowed the mobile and zipped his jacket. The wind snatched drops of blood from his torn knuckle, carried them into the Honda's slipstream. He imagined Luka and Anton following his trail, tracking the blood like breadcrumbs through a forest.

He thought about what he'd do to Hazbi Dunja when he finally had the bastard alone. Well, not quite alone. There was the woman, too. Even when he'd finished with Dunja, there'd be plenty left to occupy him.

At last he spotted the taxi, less than a hundred metres away. It had slowed to ninety. Dunja was getting complacent. That was fine by Milos: Anton would catch them up all the sooner.

He throttled back to match the taxi's speed. Another bridge went past. When the taxi emerged from beneath its shadow, sunlight splashed its roof. Ahead, green fields swelled out of the dissolving mist. The land ahead looked clean and fine, almost magical.

He thought again about his father's old bike. This time the memory was of it mangled beneath the tracks of a Croat tank. That had been afterwards. After the soldiers had broken into the house, brandishing their machine guns and shouting their obscenities. After they'd trapped Milos' family in the little front room, surrounded by the broken crockery they'd raked from the shelves. After Dunja had finished his business. When there'd only been Milos left.

He'd run out of the trees where he'd been hiding,

across the paddock, his vision blurred with tears. The last tank had already vanished down the narrow road leading north out of town. The soldiers had gone. And there had been his father's bike, flattened out like a soft tin toy, fuel tank crushed and empty, NSU badge mashed in the kerosene mud. The wheel spokes jutting like broken fingers.

Perhaps that would be a good place to start his work: by breaking Dunja's fingers.

Fate, he thought, as he pursued his quarry into the sunlight on a Honda that felt like a winged horse. *It always catches you in the end. So said my father.*

7

March 1st
12:11
Cabinet Office, Whitehall

HENRY kept both his back and face straight as he marched to his office through the gloomy Whitehall corridors. It was his father's legacy, he knew, this obsession with deportment.

'Stand tall, Henry,' his father had lectured. 'Shoulders back. Never let them see you're beaten.'

Later in life, he'd taken up archery in an effort to do something his father *didn't* approve of (Henry Worthington Senior was a rugby man; his longshanks son hated contact sports). After just ten minutes tuition in how to hold the bow and a whole ten hours in how to stand properly, he quickly realised he'd chosen a sport where the key is good posture.

'Stand straight,' the coach had urged, tapping Henry in the small of the back. 'Imagine you've got a dictionary balanced on your head. And keep your shoulders back.'

That was the moment he'd given in, accepted he was his father's son and concentrated on putting all the arrows in the gold.

All the same, it was hard to walk tall when you'd just had your balls broken.

Henry was on his way back from a meeting with his boss Oliver Fleet, the Security and Intelligence Coordinator. Oliver was no happier with Henry than the Permanent Secretary, who'd also been present. Between them they'd made it clear that if Henry didn't scoop up this particular pile of dog shit before the press got a sniff of it, they'd spike his head on Traitor's Gate.

'And you told me things had settled down after the DPG merger,' Oliver had said, sadly shaking his head. 'I trust you're going to be able to deal with this cock-up without needing to form yet another new department.'

You told me...

You're going to deal with it...

Oliver Fleet was good at reminding his staff when their heads were on the block. He was just as good at keeping his own head off it. Everyone called him Teflon behind his back, and he knew it. Somehow, however much mud got slung at him, none of it ever stuck.

Henry could take Oliver's slipperiness. He was more bothered by the Permanent Secretary, who said little, just stood behind Oliver, looking stern. His presence meant the Prime Minister was already aware of the Dunja crisis—and was paying close attention. Not good.

Henry spent most of the meeting playing things down. The situation had arisen due to events entirely out of their control: the fog, Hazbi Dunja's unexpected dash from Stansted, yes, a Croatian diplomat was missing, but a crack SOD unit was on the case, had probably caught up with Dunja already, in fact. They would soon get things back on track. Such emergencies were even use-ful, to prove the efficiency of Britain's international security services. One might even look on it as a 'live' training exercise.

Henry's back had been ramrod straight as he'd poured honey over his superiors. Secretly, he'd been asking himself the same question over and over again:

Why is this happening to me?

Oliver had dismissed him with a slick smile and a suggestion that Henry keep him updated through the course of the day.

'As soon as *you've* devised *your* solution,' he'd said, 'be sure and let me know what *you're* going to do.'

The Permanent Secretary, still silent, had nodded and smiled the smile of a viper.

Henry turned into the long south gallery and picked up his pace. There was a lot to do. He was eager to be back in his office, where he could convince himself he was in control.

The worst of it was that Oliver Fleet was right: it *was* all down to him.

At this time of day the sun should have been lancing into the gallery from the courtyard. But all he could see through the tall windows was the fog, thicker now and dark, like steel wool. He turned through the double doors and marched straight past Eileen's desk. Sensing his mood, she kept her head down.

He slammed the door behind him.

The office calmed him. It always did. His haven. The ticking clock on the mantelpiece. The Stubbs racehorses on the walls. He treated himself to a single shot of malt whisky and drank half. He stood, cradling the whisky tumbler, and stared through the window at the fog.

The telephone shattered the peace. Henry returned to

his desk, picked up the phone and said, 'Worthington.' He hoped it was good news.

'Funny old world, isn't it?' It was Jack McClintock again. With a grimace, Henry downed the rest of his drink. 'I just paid a visit to your gaff. Didn't come in, of course. Shame really—I could've dropped in on you.'

God forbid, thought Henry.

'Anyway, who should I spot but our dear old Foreign Secretary all dressed up with nowhere to go. I've never seen a man so occupied with twiddling his thumbs. And to cap it all, there were all those happy snappers wanting to know when they were going to get their pictures. So how about it, Henry? Where the hell's this tame Croatian of yours?'

'Quiet news day is it, Jack?' said Henry.

'Not any more! Spill the beans, Henry. What's going on?'

'I'm sorry to have to break this to you, Jack, but have you ever heard the expression, "No news is good news"? Well, that's all I've got for you: no news. Everything is fully under control. So if you'll just…'

'If everything's under control, why did the Foreign Secretary look like the only girl at the prom without a partner? Come on, Henry—we all know Dunja's missed his first slot of the day. Will he turn up for the rest? What about Scotland tomorrow? There are cracks in the plaster, Henry. Don't pretend you can paper over them…'

While Jack badgered, Henry's eyes strayed to his desk calendar. He was having lunch with Jack and Mary on Sunday. Maybe he'd take his sister aside after the meal, ask her to have a word with her oh-so-irritating husband. Remind him there was a line between backing the family and taking the piss.

'...so I got to thinking,' Jack was saying, 'what with Dunja's plane getting diverted and everything, maybe you've had a few security hiccups? You've heard the travel reports, I daresay? All the roads in-bound from Stansted gridlocked. No harm in telling me your man's stuck in traffic, is there?'

Henry had been about to hang up. Now he started paying attention. Jack wasn't firing blind—he'd obviously got some kind of lead on things. 'I won't deny the diversion of Mr Dunja's flight from Heathrow to Stansted has upset our itinerary today,' he said. He kept his voice smooth; the whisky helped. 'But all feasts are moveable.'

'Hard to keep a lid on security under these circumstances, though. Or so I'd imagine.'

'You can imagine what you like, Jack. The fact is, there's no story for you here.'

'Only I can't help wondering about this new unit of yours—the SODs. You pulled that merger off smoothly enough, but there are still a few little birdies talking about ruffled feathers. You know the birdies I mean, don't you, Henry?'

Henry silently cursed the gods of Fleet Street. Six months ago, when he'd been frantically spinning all the plates he needed to get the merger through, Jack McClintock had been a useful ally. He'd happily lapped up the 'confidential' information Henry had dripped out to him and dutifully delivered sympathetic copy in *The Times*. Now the whole business was coming back to bite him.

'Listen to me, Jack. As you well know, SOD's operational response is exactly the same as it was when it was the Diplomatic Protection Group. Better in fact. Things haven't changed nearly as much as you think. We went through all this at the time.'

'Middle management still happy? I always got the impression they weren't. Too much autonomy given to the officers on the ground, some said. Which starts me wondering: do those autonomous officers get confused when planes get diverted?'

'As I've already told you, Jack, the situation at Heathrow has made a dent in our timetable, nothing more.'

'Hmm. Just a couple more questions, Henry. You don't mind, do you?'

Jack continued to pump away. Henry continued to feed him what he thought of as the standard bread and water diet for journalists: something to fill the belly but not arouse the taste buds. All Jack could make from this was copy so bland it would never make it past the sub-editor.

Then Jack stopped him dead.

'I've been digging a bit deeper into that Operation Thunder business in Croatia. Wall-to-wall atrocities, really nasty stuff. Radical cleansing of every settlement on the main Serb evacuation route. Whole towns razed to the ground, regardless of whether the people had fled or not. Not something you'd ever forget. Maybe even something you'd rather hide. Either way, something that'd stay with you the rest of your life.'

'I don't know where you've been getting your information…'

'Just digging, Henry. It's what I do best. Anyway, it seems your man Dunja was right in the thick of it. But for all his war stories, Operation Thunder isn't something he ever talks about. Funny, that. And here's the good bit: fast-forward from the war and what do we find? Our former tank commander goes AWOL on what's probably the most important visit of his diplomatic career so far. Maybe I'm crazy, but you know what, Henry? I think there's a gaping hole in Dunja's life story. You know me and my hunches. I think your precious foreign minister might have an agenda we don't know about.'

There were two phones on Henry's desk. He was just wondering—again—why he'd been foolish enough to give Jack McClintock his direct number, when the red light on the second phone started flashing. The light meant a call on his secure line—a number he would never give to a man like Jack in a million years.

'I'm sorry, Jack,' he said. All the smoothness had left his voice. Boy, did he need another whisky! 'You'll have to navigate la-la-land by yourself. I have an awful lot to get through this morning.'

He hung up without saying goodbye.

'Worthington!' he snapped into the other phone.

'Henry, Brian. I think we've got…'

'I *know* what we've got, Brian!' Henry said. He imagined Chief Superintendent Burfield recoiling at the other end and the image brought him grim satisfaction. 'We've got a situation that's rapidly spiralling out of control. I've just had my bollocks chewed off by the Permanent Secretary and if you don't get a grip on things those same bollocks are due to be served up to the Prime Minister on a silver platter for tea. And as if that isn't enough, I've got the press snapping at my heels wanting an exclusive on a story that doesn't look like it's going to have a happy ending.'

'If you'll just let me…'

'Let you what? Bang another nail in the coffin of the DPG? You're the one who fought for change, Brian. *This merger's just what we need.* That's what you told me.

Things can only get better. The merger was your baby and I supported you all the way. Don't tell me I've backed a three-legged horse. And don't pretend you want to be riding one. So I'll tell you what I want you to do. I want you to prove to me that SOD is the thoroughbred you're always telling me it is. I want you to prove to me that your officers are capable of fighting this fire before it starts blazing out of control. I want you to justify the faith I've put in you and your department time and time again. And above all, I want you to tell me WHERE THE FUCK IS HAZBI DUNJA?'

Silence on the other end of the line. Maybe Burfield had fallen off his chair. Or had a stroke. Henry took in a deep breath, let it out slowly.

'Brian?' he said. 'Are you still there?'

'Uh, yes. Look, sorry, Henry, I'm going to have to call you back. Charlie Paddon's on the other line.'

'Let's hope it's good news.'

Henry slammed down the phone and treated himself to that second whisky. He felt better for letting off steam. Burfield was a bulldog but it didn't hurt to remind him who was holding the leash.

He wondered what Paddon had been calling in to report.

The fog clung to the windows. It felt as if someone had dropped a shroud over the entire building. Unconsciously, Henry straightened up in his chair. Sitting up straight helped him not to feel so powerless.

He thumbed the intercom.

'Eileen,' he said. 'Get me Nick Luard, please. Secure line, priority one.'

Time to talk to the spooks.

8

March 1st
13:42
A1 Northbound

TRAFFIC cones loomed out of the mist. Alex watched glumly as temporary signs counted down the distance to the roadworks. It was the second set they'd hit since leaving Stansted. And the weather wasn't getting any better.

And, for whatever reason, it seemed Hazbi Dunja didn't want to be stopped.

The whole journey had been like this. It wasn't just London that was fogbound. All the way north Alex and Charlie had been following a trail of half-sightings and failed pursuits. South of Grantham the Lincolnshire traffic police had picked up the minicab, actually got on its tail for a while. But the cab had left the A1 for a while, snuck around the back roads, and the local cops had lost it. Their chopper was grounded so they'd had to fall back on old-fashioned eyeballing. It had been just enough to confirm the cab's eventual return to its original route.

That had been over half an hour ago, with no sightings since. Alex hoped the trail hadn't gone cold.

An Ikea lorry thundered past, bent on overtaking them before the road narrowed. Spray erupted across the windscreen. Alex gripped the seat as Charlie nudged the BMW in to give the idiot room, his hands tight on the wheel. The car responded smoothly. Much as she teased him, Alex admired the way he handled the car.

'I can't believe how far they've dragged us,' she said. 'Where the hell are they?'

'We'll catch them.' The determined look on Charlie's face gave Alex some welcome reassurance.

They passed a pair of yellow Motorway Maintenance vehicles. Just beyond them, a road sign told them they were entering South Yorkshire. 'We have officially reached The North,' said Alex.

'Crikey,' said Charlie, 'is that Sherwood Forest been and gone already?'

'If it was, I blinked and missed it.'

'You've got to feel sorry for Robin Hood. Poor bastard's only got three scruffy pine trees to hide behind these days.'

'Times change. I hear the current Sheriff's a woman. That's got to spice things up a bit.'

'Says you. I tell you what though: at this rate we won't be home for tea. Looks like you'll be reading Fraser his bedtime story over the phone.'

'Danni puts him on loudspeaker,' said Alex. 'He loves it.'

'Bet you won't miss doing the nappies.'

'Fraser's almost three, Charlie. We have so done nappies.'

Not only was he potty-trained, but Alex's son could also work most of the household gadgets better than she could. Including the phones. Her husband Lawrie liked to joke he was the next logical step in human evolution.

Alex checked her watch. Charlie was right. It didn't look like she'd be back in her house in Brentford until after dark. Plus she had to be up early for the flight to Edinburgh. Tomorrow morning Dunja was due to address the Scottish Parliament. It was their job to protect him while he did so. Of course, they had to find him first.

She hoped she'd be able to get her call in to Fraser before he went to sleep. It made all the difference on the days she didn't get home before his bedtime. Especially now Lawrie was working in Aberdeen.

One reason Alex got on so well with Charlie was he didn't keep asking her how she managed to juggle career with family. Everyone asked her that—even Lawrie. It was such a drag.

Charlie was different. He didn't hassle her about it at all. He understood she lived her life this way for one simple reason: because she wanted to. The beauty was, it actually worked. Danni the nanny (how she and Lawrie had laughed about *that* one after the interview) was a dream and Fraser loved the idea that his mummy was a 'peacelady'. Somehow it all just seemed to hang together.

As usual, Charlie had a way of summing it up: 'You're just a Zen-chick, aren't you?'

Alex didn't know about that. But she did pride herself on trying to live for the present. How else could a working mother allow herself to speed north in pursuit of a lost diplomat while her son was home playing pat-a-cake with the live-in nanny and her husband was off designing oil pipelines in Aberdeen?

As the A1 took them past Blythe services, a call came in on Alex's radio.

'This could be them,' she said. She relayed the information to Charlie. 'A minicab—a blue Skoda—just

tripped the speed cameras on another set of roadworks...
uh, south of Doncaster. Not humping it, just lazy pedals—
forty on a thirty stretch. The fog obscured the plates but
they've got a partial on the phone number. It matches
what we know.'

'It's our day for thumbs on the lens,' said Charlie.
'But that sounds like our man.'

As they cleared the roadworks, Charlie floored the
accelerator. Doncaster wasn't far. At last they were getting somewhere.

'Hold on,' said the police operator. 'This might not
mean anything but a second vehicle's just come up on the
same camera. A motorbike, also doing forty, same as the
minicab. Yellow fuel tank, plate obscured. Sounds like the
same chap one of our patrols spotted earlier. Nothing
untoward, it's just he isn't wearing any gloves. Hardly il-
legal, but not exactly comfortable at this time of year.'

Alex thanked her and ended the call.

'What d'you think?' she said.

'I think it's the second time today we've heard about
funny business with a motorbike.'

'The despatch rider at the airport?'

Charlie nodded. Alex grinned. It felt good when they
were tuned to the same station.

'Get on to that idiot at Stansted,' Charlie said. 'Gromit,
or whatever his name was.'

'Wallace.'

While she was putting in the call, Alex couldn't help
noticing the speedometer was up to one-ten. The fields
flew past the windows. She could read the excitement in
Charlie's face. It was the same as what she could feel at
the base of her belly. They were closing in.

Sergeant Wallace was eager to make up for his failure

to detain Dunja. He lost no time in pulling up the despatch
rider's description of the man who'd stolen his bike.

'I don't know if it'll help,' he said. 'Chap says it all happened so quickly. How many times have you heard that?'

'Just give me what you've got,' said Alex.

'Okay…we've got heavy build, dark hair, swarthy
complexion…'

'Sounds interesting,' said Alex. She fished Burfield's
fax out of the glove box. The BMW hit a bumpy patch
of road and she nearly dropped it. Slamming the glove
box shut, she studied the picture at the bottom of the
page: a bearded Javor Milos stared out at her from a field
of broken pixels. 'What about facial hair?'

'No, he was clean-shaven.'

'Oh.'

'But it's funny you should ask.'

'Why?' Alex raised her eyebrows at Charlie.

'Well, our despatch fellow mentioned this swarthy
complexion, but he went on to say the bloke's chin looked
pale. And there were a couple of scabs. Like he'd just…'

'…shaved off his beard,' said Alex. 'Thank you,
Sergeant Wallace. You've been a tremendous help.'

She rang off, waved the fax in triumph. 'It's him. It's
got to be.'

'Agreed,' said Charlie. 'This might explain why
Dunja's so keen to keep on the move. Wouldn't you, with
a professional hit man on your tail?'

The road widened to four lanes. Charlie made the
most of it, swinging out and punching on the blues and
twos. The BMW sped briefly into mist then out into watery sunlight.

'Let's think this through,' said Alex. She read through
the fax again. 'If this gloveless biker really is Javor Milos…'

'It is.'

'Well, we don't know for sure, but we've got to assume the worst. If it is him, then Dunja's in real danger. What I don't get is how Milos picked up his trail so fast. MI6 are telling us Milos was already in the country, probably under a false passport, in which case he must have been waiting for Dunja at Heathrow, just like we were. But with the plane getting diverted like that…I can't believe anyone could've got round the M25 to Stansted quicker than we did. How did he get ahead of us?'

'Maybe the spooks got it wrong,' said Charlie. His eyes were wide, intent on the road. 'Maybe Milos wasn't in the country at all.'

'What do you mean?'

'Maybe he was on the plane.'

Minutes later, Alex was talking to Brian Burfield. Charlie had spoken to him earlier, keeping him posted on their progress up the country. At the time, Brian had still been smarting from Henry Worthington's verbal assault. Now, when he heard Alex's news, he pulled his natural pessimism back a notch or two. In fact, he almost sounded cheerful. For Brian.

'If you're right,' he said, 'it proves those wankers at MI6 aren't half as clever as they think.'

'So you'll check the passenger list?' said Alex, trying to keep him on track.

'Yes, yes, of course. I tell you what though, Alex, nothing would give me greater pleasure than to see that supercilious git Nick Luard squirming in front of Henry bloody Worthington. It's about time someone brought him down a peg or two. Why they put him in charge of MI6 I'll never know. It's hard enough handling these foreigners without throwing a backstabber like him into the mix.'

Alex performed the difficult task of ending the conversation without actually hanging up on her boss.

'All right, here we go,' she said, when she'd finally succeeded. She held up her right hand, thumb extended. 'One: Milos is on the plane, which explains why he's at Stansted and we're not.'

'Check,' said Charlie.

She stuck out her index finger. 'Two: Dunja knows Milos is at large and makes sure he gets out of the airport as quickly as he can. Wait—strike that. What if he actually spots Milos while they're disembarking? He sees Milos, gets scared and makes a run for it?'

'Could be. But don't forget Dunja was expecting to be picked up by SOD. All right, he probably guessed we'd been snookered by the diversion, but that still doesn't explain why he didn't hand himself over to the airport police as soon as he got to customs.'

'Maybe he didn't trust them to keep him safe. He must know Milos will stop at nothing. Even getting himself arrested so he can share the same custody suite as the man he wants to kill.'

'But why get in a minicab, for God's sake? Something's still not right.'

'And why drive all the way to Yorkshire?' said Alex, looking out through the window. The four lanes had narrowed back to three. Charlie kept the sirens going. Cars pulled in to let them pass.

'Never mind Yorkshire. At this rate we'll be in Scotland for tea.'

'Edinburgh?' said Alex, eyebrows raised. 'As in Holyrood?'

'I don't know. Like I said—something doesn't add up.'

While he coaxed a little more speed out of the BMW,

Alex got back in touch with the Doncaster police, told them to alert the local traffic cops. It was vital they flagged down Dunja before Milos caught up with him. Vital, too, that Milos be approached only with extreme caution.

'There's every chance he's armed,' she told the sergeant at the other end. 'You deal with Dunja. Leave the assassin to us.'

They drove on in silence for a moment. Trees flashed past, leafless and wintry.

'How far to Doncaster?' Alex said at last.

'Not far,' said Charlie. 'Let's hope we make it without having to fill up.' Alex leaned over to peer at the fuel gauge, which was edging into the red. 'Alex—when we catch them, let's be careful.'

'Always.'

'We want the same thing Milos wants: Hazbi Dunja. The only difference is we want him alive.'

'Milos will be armed.'

'Then it's a good job we are, too.'

'Think it'll come to that?'

'Let's just hope he's a poor shot.'

9

March 1st
14:09
A1 Northbound

THE SILVER Jaguar hung in Milos's rear-view mirror. Milos briefly raised his frozen right hand. The Jaguar's nose lifted. It nudged forward, swept alongside him.

On the car's dashboard, a blue light started to flash.

He been watching the Jaguar in his mirror for five minutes before the text message had finally come through. He'd been beginning to wonder if it really was an unmarked police car. There were two men in the front, but the car didn't come close enough for him to see their faces. The damn fog didn't help. Then his mobile had buzzed.

The message confirmed it was Anton behind the wheel. The passenger was Luka, Milos had never been more pleased to see anyone. The kilometres had chipped away at his mood. And his hands were starting to hurt like fuck.

SERVICE STATION, the message had read. *10K. WE MOVE.*

Milos had waved his hand to signal approval. Anton

had flashed the Jaguar's headlamps in acknowledgement, and hung back until the moment was right. That moment was now.

The road ahead was clear. That was good. Anton would need room to manoeuvre. After cruising beside the Honda for a few seconds, the Jaguar pulled ahead. Milos surged into the Jaguar's slipstream, head low, no longer aware of the pain in his fingers. The taxi's tail lights, burning red, grew steadily bigger.

A blue sign signalled two miles to Robin Hood Services. Milos felt momentarily disorientated. Surely Nottingham was many kilometres behind them? It didn't matter. The Jaguar was closing in on the taxi, the light on the dashboard stabbing blue blades through the fog. There was no way Dunja could miss it.

Milos kept his distance, let the little drama play itself out.

One mile to go.

Anton pulled out into the middle lane, drew alongside the taxi. To the casual eye, the two men in the Jaguar could pass for plain-clothes cops.

Milos twisted the throttle and closed the gap. He saw Luka waggle his hand and point, telling the driver of the taxi to pull over. The taxi showed no sign of slowing down. Milos checked his speedometer: 110kph. The taxi weaved for a moment, then started pulling away. The driver had put his foot to the floor.

Anton followed suit. The Skoda was no match for the big Jaguar. Again, Luka waved. The taxi started weaving again; its exhaust coughed blue smoke. Anton heeled the Jaguar to the left, crossing the white line and forcing the taxi over towards the hard shoulder. The taxi dropped back. Anton matched its speed precisely, following its every move.

They passed a sign with three white bars—the start of the countdown to the service station slip road.

The taxi's nearside wheels clipped the rumble strip at the edge of the inside lane. It swerved towards the Jaguar, then veered back at the last minute. The Jaguar edged further to the left, forcing the taxi all the way on to the hard shoulder. They passed the sign with two white lines. Ahead, looming out of the fog, was the exit ramp. The ramp rose steeply to the level of the service station bridge.

The taxi's brake lights came on. The driver was trying to regain the carriageway by dodging behind the Jaguar. Milos found himself closing rapidly. Instinctively, he reached for his own brakes: he wasn't keen on ploughing into the back of the Skoda. The taxi swerved right but Anton's reflexes were flawless. He'd already braked and the Jaguar was right there, blocking the way. The taxi's brake lights went off. They were down to sixty kph.

A sign with one bar. The exit ramp was on them. Yet again, the taxi swung out. For a moment, Milos thought it was going straight through Anton and back on to the carriageway. But the carriageway wasn't there any more, just the massive concrete bridge support. Dunja had left it too late. There was nowhere else to go but into the service station.

Losing speed at a steady rate, Anton shadowed the taxi up the exit ramp. Milos followed, dropping through the gears. All the numbness had left him. The pain of the kilometres had fallen away. The only thing that mattered now was revenge. He didn't even care about the woman. If he didn't get her, that was okay. He just wanted Dunja.

The two cars moved into the sliproad marked for automobiles and snaked into the carpark. To the left was a small, shabby mall; beside the mall was a motel. Directly ahead was a petrol station, glowing in the fog like a grounded UFO. The taxi had slowed to a crawl. Milos was closing fast. He could see Luka and Anton getting ready to jump out of the Jaguar. The blue light was still flashing. Anton's door started swinging open. Milos's heartbeat stepped up a gear.

The taxi lunged forward, tyres squealing. It swung in front of the Jaguar, heading straight for the petrol station. If it got through, it would have a clear run down the far ramp and back on to the motorway. Anton slammed his door shut again, prepared to give chase…and stalled the car.

The taxi shot through the lurid glare of the petrol station canopy. It swerved through the pumps. A young woman in a short skirt was filling up a black Audi. She stared open-mouthed as the taxi squealed past her, inches from one shapely hip.

Milos opened up the Honda. He roared past the stalled Jaguar, front wheel rising briefly off the tarmac, skidding past the woman with the short skirt and the Audi. A man who'd just finished refuelling his Toyota jumped aside. The hose he'd been holding dropped to the ground like a dead snake.

He slalomed through the pumps and caught up with the taxi just as it reached the top of the exit ramp. A lorry emerged from the truckers' park at the back of the petrol station and cut in front of them both. The taxi braked hard, skewing sideways Instinctively, Milos looped to the side and aimed the bike straight at the driver's door.

The Honda's front wheel hit the door with a colossal *crump*. The shock sent shotgun blasts up Milos's arms and his hands jumped off the grips. As the bike folded under him he piled into the side of the taxi, bounced off, hit the ground hard on his shoulder. His head snapped back as the helmet crunched onto the tarmac. The impact hammered the breath from his lungs. He rolled, and tucked his legs in just in time to stop them being smashed by the falling bike. The taxi spun away from him, drifting on to the grass verge to face back the way it had come. Through the taxi's front window he saw the driver—a man he didn't recognise—bounce off the inside of the door jamb, blood pouring from a gash on the side of his head. The taxi sat on the grass, motionless.

Milos lay there on his side, gasping for breath. It felt like all the ribs on his left side were broken, and the knock to the head sent a spasm of nausea through his stomach. The Honda was on its side, too, front wheel spinning horizontally just centimetres from his cracked visor. He felt the ground rumble beneath him, and raised his head to see the Jaguar scream past. Tyres squealing, it came to a halt right next to the taxi. This time the taxi didn't pull away.

Luka was first out, closely followed by Anton. Milos watched Anton slide across the bonnet and decided he'd seen too much American TV. The two men yanked open the taxi's rear doors. Luka reached in and started pulling out the woman. She clawed her hands down Luka's face; she was as feisty as Milos had imagined she might be. The discovery sent a shiver down his spine. He flipped the woman round, grabbed her hair, and clamped his arm across her breasts. She kicked Luka's shins, jabbed her elbows into his belly. But Luka was strong, and carried her as if she were a child. Anton had reached the taxi's other door just in time to stop Dunja making a dash for it.

Milos was on his knees now, peering over the smashed Honda. His breathing had returned to normal and, though his ribs ached, he didn't think they were broken. Time to join his comrades. But, as he stood, he heard more squealing. Somewhere close by, someone else was burning rubber.

A black Range Rover raced from the behind the jet wash. The windows were tinted, the plates obscured with hastily applied paint. Twenty metres from the stricken Honda it skidded to a halt. The driver jumped out. He was holding an automatic rifle.

Milos dropped. A bullet clipped the Honda's front forks; two more buried themselves in the saddle. The whipcrack sounds of the gunshots died without echo. He crawled on his belly to the back of the bike, peered under the rear wheel. The rifleman was down on one knee. A fourth bullet skimmed the tarmac centimetres from Milos's outstretched hand. He snatched his arm back and curled himself, trying to make himself as small a target as possible.

Milos glanced across at the other cars. Anton, his own gun drawn, had hustled Dunja round behind the Jaguar. Luka bundled the woman—who'd given up struggling for now—on to the back seat and slammed the door on her. Milos heard two more shots. The rear window of the taxi exploded.

So did the back of Luka's head. Instantly his body went limp. Blood spraying from the hole in his skull, he folded out of sight behind the Jaguar.

Milos wanted to stand up, to shout and scream. Ten years he'd known Luka. But if he screamed he'd be as dead as his friend. Keeping low, he eased off his helmet, put it gently on the ground. A few metres behind him was a grass verge dotted with bushes. As long as the rifleman stayed distracted, he could use the bushes as cover to reach the Jaguar.

He started crawling.

A bullet hit the Honda's fuel tank. A bang filled Milos' head, then the whole world caught fire.

Milos scrambled backwards on his hands and heels, the hot stench of burning petrol crashing over him like a breaking wave. The rough ground tore skin from the palms of his hands. The flames beat against his face. Black smoke boiled skywards, beating back the fog. He listened for more shots, then realised he couldn't hear anything at all: the explosion had rendered him temporarily deaf.

But the flames had provided him with far better cover than a line of scraggy bushes.

He poised himself like a sprinter, cold and bleeding knuckles pressed against the tarmac. Then he ran.

The taxi was only ten metres away. He had no idea if he was being fired on. It didn't matter. If he was hit he'd know it soon enough. He saw Anton waving him on.

'Get Dunja!' he yelled. His own words sounded like distant cries. At least he could hear them—his eardrums were recovering, slowly.

Anton shouted something Milos couldn't make out. A bullet snapped off the taxi's rear bumper. Luckily, the taxi was positioned so as to form a shield between the rifleman and the Jaguar. Milos tripped as he reached it, fell heavily, dragged himself into the gap between the two cars. There was a pause, then both the taxi's rear tyres blew out as bullets hammered into them.

Milos lay there, breathing hard. Looking up, he saw Dunja and the woman in the back of the Jaguar. Anton was in the driver's seat, leaning backwards with his gun pressed against Dunja's temple. Dunja looked haggard, the woman defiant. Neither prisoner moved.

Anton beckoned Milos into the car. They were going to make it.

Who the hell was the mystery man was in the Range Rover? MI5? Milos inched towards the Jaguar's passenger door. Just as Anton threw it open for him, he glanced behind him.

The last thing he expected to see was yet another vehicle piling on to the scene. The newcomer roared into the petrol station and came to an abrupt halt just beyond the last pump in line. This new car's livery was unmistakeable.

It was a red police BMW.

10

March 1ˢᵗ
14:11
Cabinet Office, Whitehall

WHILE Eileen showed his visitors in, Henry stood with his face to the window and his back to the door. A touch dramatic, he supposed. But this was likely to be something of a circus, and he was keen to remind the performers that he was the ringmaster.

'Brian,' he said. 'Nick.'

He turned to face them. To his dismay, the two men were ignoring him, in favour of glowering at each other.

'Sit down,' he snapped. 'Both of you. You've got a lot of explaining to do.'

Brian Burfield slumped in the nearer of the two chairs Henry had set out. Nick Luard looked down his nose at the remaining seat, brushed imaginary dust from the cushion and sat down.

The two men looked like mismatched bookends. Burfield—as short as Luard was tall—sank in the plush upholstery. He looked altogether out of place in Henry's immaculate office: a beggar at the feast. Despite his Chief

Superintendent's uniform, he looked ever the working class hero.

Luard, in contrast, looked entirely at home, and suave to boot. While his suit wasn't as expensive as Henry's, he had a maddening way of wearing it like he didn't care. He studied the paraphernalia on Henry's desk, as if playing the parlour game where you memorise everything on a tray for later recollection. Or maybe he was just looking for dust.

'I really don't know why you had to bring us both in, Henry,' said Luard. 'MI6 doesn't run itself, you know. I do have other responsibilities.'

'Oh, that's right,' said Burfield, before Henry could reply. 'Do the usual hit and run, why don't you? Make the mess, then leave the rest of us to clear it up.'

'Brian, I'm sure I don't know what you mean.' Luard looked away, nose in the air.

'Yes, you do. The first I heard about Javor Milos was during this morning's briefing. Even then it was only mentioned in passing. I had to call your boys myself to get all the details. By the time I got the fax out to Charlie Paddon, Flight 312 was already on its way to Stansted.'

'Faxes now, Brian? I thought you were still using carrier pigeons.'

'Don't push me, Nick. The fact is your department was late with its information, as usual. But that's not the half of it. Do you want to know what really bugs me?'

'I'm sure you'll tell me.'

'It's obvious Milos has been building his UK network for months. I'm willing to bet he's been in and out of this country on any number of false passports since before Christmas. I'm also willing to bet his movements have more than a little to do with the curious spate of murders we've been witnessing lately. You know—all those citizens of the former Yugoslavia who keep turning up face-down in the Thames?'

'Naturally, there's a big picture,' said Luard. 'A lot bigger than you realise, in fact. But why don't you let us worry about that, Brian? Your force is called "Metropolitan" for a reason, you know.'

'Why you…'

Henry rapped on the desk. 'Children, please,' he said. 'If you want to fight, do it in the playground afterwards.'

'He started it,' said Luard, with an agreeable smile.

'I've brought you here,' Henry persisted, 'to work *together*, not tear each other's throats out. We need to salvage something from this debacle.'

The two men glared at each other. Henry wondered if he ought to acquire a whip. This would be the perfect moment to crack one.

'Brian,' he said, steepling his fingers, 'I'd rather hoped you'd be able to kick things off. You're closest to what's happening on the ground.'

'I am,' said Burfield, 'and we'll get to that. But there's more going on here than just the current crisis, Henry.' His face was pink. His hands gripped the arms of the chair. 'This could be the thin end of the wedge. If Milos can get away with pulling a stunt like this it opens the floodgates. Suddenly, the UK becomes a handy arena where any old Johnny Foreigner can bring his grudges— not to mention his shooting irons—to exact a bit of petty vengeance. Which is exactly why MI6 need to pull their bloody fingers out and start providing us with decent intelligence. Starting with who these people are and where they come from. *Before* they turn up on our doorstep.'

Nick Luard said nothing, just continued to smile.

'Thank you, Brian, for that highly analytical tirade,' said Henry. 'Nick, have you got anything to add before we actually start a serious debate?'

'Well,' said Luard. 'I feel I must point out that while MI6 is indeed responsible for providing intelligence, it is up to SOD to act on it. I'm sure even you, Brian, will agree it was not MI6 that was responsible for allowing a visiting Croatian diplomat to walk unescorted out of an international airport, climb into a minicab and travel unchallenged over two hundred miles up the country.'

'We're in pursuit,' muttered Burfield.

'The way your luck's going, that little BMW will probably run out of petrol before you even get near.'

Henry watched Burfield slouch deeper into his chair. If he were a volcano, he'd be smoking.

'But it's not *all* Brian's fault,' Luard went on.

Burfield didn't rise to that, but Henry raised his eyebrows. 'What do you mean?' he said.

'We have to ask ourselves why a man like Hazbi Dunja was allowed to enter the country in the first place. With his dubious war record, his reputation in the media as a poacher turned gamekeeper and his highly questionable attitude to human rights—particularly the rights of ethnic minorities in his own country it's a wonder the man ever made it on to your department's approved list. The decision to admit him lies far outside the jurisdiction of MI6. Henry—you have to acknowledge the fact that Hazbi Dunja is only in the country because you sent him an invitation.'

The grim smile on Brian Burfield's face infuriated Henry almost as much as Nick Luard's unprovoked attack. But, to his surprise, it was Burfield who came to his defence.

'Croatia's had a recognised parliament since 2000,'

said the dour Chief Superintendent. 'Of course they want to join the party. As long as they bring a bottle, we have to make them welcome. The war's over, the Reds have gone to hide under someone else's bed. Times change.'

'Been reading up, have we?' said Luard.

'More than you might think.'

'When was the last time you actually visited the Balkans?'

'When was the last time you actually visited the real world?'

To Henry's relief, the phone rang. He'd left Eileen strict instructions not to disturb him, so it had to be important.

He took the call.

'Eileen's got one of your people on the line,' he said to Burfield when he'd put the phone down. 'Sergeant Chappell. Take it in the next office, please, Brian. There are a few things I need to discuss with Nick. Report back when you're done.'

Burfield left the room.

Henry stood, returned to the window. It was all very well being ringmaster. The trouble was the clowns just never did as they were told.

It wasn't so much that Burfield and Luard disliked each other. They were just so defensive. All they'd done since coming in the room was cover their own arses. Well, Henry knew all about self-preservation. He'd practically elevated it to an art form. In others, though, it wasn't such an attractive trait.

Nick Luard angered him most. The man's cavalier approach to national security was highly questionable. On the other hand, he had to admire Luard's front. He understood the Whitehall game and played it as well as any politician. Or bureaucrat.

He'd fit in here very well, Henry mused.

Burfield was different. Unlike Luard, he was genuinely interested in people. Especially in their ability to screw up. He was well-read and he was canny. Which was exactly what made him extraordinarily good at his job.

It was ironic: where Henry knew exactly what made Nick Luard tick, he no more understood Brian Burfield than he would a man from Mars. But if he had to choose one of the two to watch his back, he'd pick Burfield every time.

'We're going to have to go public, Nick,' he said. 'Otherwise God knows what fairy stories we'll be reading in tonight's *Evening Standard*.'

'Yes, the media do like to take an interest,' said Luard. 'They and others. I imagine the PM has been asking, too?'

'Naturally, I'm keeping him in the loop. He's very interested, of course. He's also insisting we keep the Croatian President fully informed every step of the way.'

'That'll go down well in Zagreb.'

'That's what I wanted to discuss with you. I need you to talk to your people over there. But tread carefully. Play it down. I don't need to tell you how sensitive relations have been since that incident last year with the Serbian asylum seekers. We need to keep our Embassy staff abreast of the situation, but it's vital they don't start shouting from the rooftops. There might be a backlash.'

'A backlash? What do you imagine, Henry—a mob of Croatians marching on the British Embassy? No doubt carrying torches and getting ready to throw nooses over every convenient tree branch?'

'Don't be facetious.'

'No, but really, Henry, you don't seriously think the Embassy is under threat of attack? Just because one of their politicians is missing?'

'I don't think anything, Nick. I merely point out possible risks. It's up to you to deal with them.'

Luard sighed. Henry kept his attention on the window. The sigh, he knew, would be accompanied by a sneer. That wasn't something he wanted to see.

'I'll have a word,' Luard said at last. 'Actually, it'll be quite a treat to hear old Monty's reaction when I tell him there's a senior Croatian minister on the loose in Yorkshire. When he hears about the Serbian assassin on a stolen motorbike he'll probably choke on his Meerschaum!'

The door swung open. Burfield was standing there, looking even redder than when he'd left. Henry and Luard exchanged a glance.

'News?' said Henry.

'It looks like Paddon and Chappell have caught up with our runaway.'

'About time. It should be a simple matter to bring him in,' said Luard.

Henry held his breath. The words were encouraging; the expression on Burfield's face wasn't.

'The situation is anything but simple,' said Burfield. 'I have to inform you my officers are attending an incident at a service station near Doncaster. Initial reports are that there's been an exchange of gunfire.'

'Sit down,' Henry snapped, 'and tell us exactly what's going on.'

11

March 1st
14:19
Robin Hood Services, A1

BARELY five minutes had passed since the call had come in from the Doncaster control centre:

'All units attend an incident at Robin Hood Service Station. Shots fired, repeat, shots fired…'

Neither Charlie nor Alex had said a word. They both knew what was coming next.

'…vehicles involved include a Skoda minicab previously reported as being pursued at speed by a yellow Honda 250…'

Charlie pushed the BMW as hard as he could. As he hit ninety, the fuel warning light blinked on. He ignored it—the reserve should last another twenty miles. More than enough.

He pressed his lips together and hoped he was right.

Sirens screaming, lights stabbing strobe-flashes into the fog, the BMW tore past a column of six curtain-siders. The lorries were slipstreaming, each driving scant metres from the next. They needed pulling over.

'Looks like we got us a convoy,' said Alex, as they passed the front runner.

'Ten-four, good buddy,' said Charlie. 'It's their lucky day—we've got bigger fish to fry.'

The traffic built up as they approached the services. Blue lights flickered ahead. A local traffic cop had been minutes from the scene when the call had come in. He'd slewed his car across the exit ramp to prevent other vehicles entering the services.

Good job, thought Charlie, but it turned his approach run into a nightmare.

The inside lane was jammed with cars wanting to use the services, but being waved on by the traffic cop. The outside lane was clear, but that wasn't where Charlie wanted to be. For the second time that day, he cut through chaos and on to the hard shoulder. Half the cars scattered before him; the other half just got in his way.

'They should add a section to the driving test,' he said, as he spun the wheel first left, then right. 'How to react to an emergency vehicle breathing down your neck.' A red Vauxhall dawdled across his path. He cursed, hit the brakes and missed clipping its rear bumper by a centimetre.

'There's a gap,' said Alex, pointing calmly. He'd already spotted it. A white van driver restored Charlie's faith in the species by swerving aside, forcing a line of cars out with him. Suddenly he had a clear run up the ramp. He accelerated past the traffic cop—who looked about twelve years old and frozen stiff—and into the service station.

He slowed, started cruising between the parked cars, looking round for signs of action. Three youths carrying Burger King boxes were standing beneath a statue of a hooded man drawing a bow and arrow. As the BMW rolled past they pointed towards the petrol station.

'I don't see…' he began.

'Behind the pumps,' said Alex. 'On the slip road.'

As Charlie guided the BMW through the pumps, they saw the black Range Rover. Behind its bonnet a man was crouched, an automatic rifle in his hand. A dazzling pillar of flame was painting everything a livid yellow.

Charlie's first thought when he saw the fire was of the several very large tanks filled with petrol a few feet beneath the forecourt.

Maybe this isn't the best place to park the BMW.

'It's the motorbike,' said Alex. 'It's on fire.'

In an eye blink, Charlie took in the rest of the scene. Beyond the burning bike were two more vehicles: the minicab they'd spent the whole day chasing, and a silver Jaguar. Figures—indistinct through the smoke and flames—were hustling round the latter. On the ground near the taxi was a body. Dark liquid that could only be blood lay pooled beneath the head and shoulders. The head looked horribly misshapen.

Shots rang through the mist. Beside him, Alex was already reaching for her shoulder-holster. Charlie kicked open the door, drew his MP5 from the customised door compartment. Alex flicked the safety off on her standard-issue Glock 17.

'Cover me!' he shouted.

With his finger under the trigger of the submachine gun, he leaped out and started running, half-crouched, towards the flaming motorbike. The heat from the fire prickled his face and the backs of his hands.

'Armed police!' he bellowed. 'Drop your weapon! Drop it now! Armed police…!' It was what Alex called Blitzspeak: assault your quarry with words, batter him so hard he can't think straight, in the hope that he'll simply obey.

In this case, the hope was in vain.

The rifle swung round, grew shorter in Charlie's vision. It was pointing right at him. The movement was unhurried, precise. This guy was a professional.

Charlie dipped left, away from the burning bike. A few more paces and the Range Rover's windscreen would block the rifleman's line of fire. Something whistled past his ear; a fraction of a second later he heard the deafening report of the shot.

Almost at once an answering spark kicked off the Range Rover's bonnet. The rifleman ducked. He seemed surprised that someone else was firing at him. Charlie took a knee and brought the stock to his shoulder.

Looking round, he saw Alex knelt on the tarmac behind the BMW's open passenger door. She was using the door as a shield. Her arms stuck through the open window, straight and steady. As he watched she squeezed the trigger a second time. The Glock kicked in her hand and one of the Range Rover's headlights shattered. The rifleman stayed low.

Thanks, Alex!

There were more shots. One of the figures beside the Jaguar had a handgun. Bullets ripped through the smoke, leaving long vortices in their wake. Was it Dunja firing the gun? Charlie couldn't make out faces. The rifleman whipped round and loosed three shots in the direction of the Jaguar. The figure with the handgun ducked back into the car. Somewhere an engine revved.

The rear tyre of the motorbike burst with a dull pop. Charlie shot a glance that way. Three trickles of flame were running across the ground: fuel from the wrecked motorbike, spilled and ignited, reaching out blazing orange fingers. Two of the trickles ended in shallow puddles burning harmlessly in the middle of the tarmac.

The third ended right underneath the Range Rover.

Charlie dropped, tucked and rolled, fetched up hard against the brick wall flanking the jet wash bay.

A split-second later the Range Rover's petrol tank exploded.

A hot fist punched into Charlie. He curled up, arm over his face, and felt it break over him like a wave. The shockwave hammered his ears, making his chest cavity reverberate. Something like acid drops peppered his skin. Peering through his fingers, he saw a ball of smoke rise from the Range Rover like a vast black balloon. All four wheels were off the ground. The body was peeling open. Inside it was what looked like a small sun.

Charlie turned away from the glare. When he looked back, the Range Rover was grounded on four flat tyres, burning ferociously. Several metres away, unconscious or dead, was the rifleman. Smoke rose from one sleeve of his leather jacket; the legs of his jeans were black and shredded.

He glanced across at the BMW. Alex was still poised behind the open passenger door, hands outstretched and steady, gun aimed square at the man on the ground. Not taking it for granted he was out of action. Yellow light burned in her eyes.

While the Range Rover blazed, the fire from the Honda was subsiding. Charlie was up, ignoring the pain where he'd fallen on his knee, side-stepping at speed towards the minicab. He kept his gun low across his body, barrel pointed at the ground. The cab looked empty but for a slumped shape behind the wheel. Beside it was the Jaguar. He counted three people inside.

As he ran, a shadowy figure rose up from the gap between the two vehicles. It was a man, heavy-set, clean-shaven. Momentarily, the mist and the smoke from the fires cleared. Charlie found himself looking straight into the man's eyes. Even without the beard he recognised him. It was Javor Milos.

For a second, Milos held Charlie's gaze. Then he threw himself into the Jaguar and slammed the passenger door shut behind him. Charlie raised his gun, started to shout. The Jaguar was well within range. But there was no clear shot at either Milos or the driver, and Charlie was only too aware that one of the people in the car was the very man he'd been assigned to protect. He lowered his aim and shot twice at the tyres. The hollow-tipped bullets both missed. The Jaguar mounted the steep bank with two wheels, sending up a shower of sparks. Charlie gave chase. By the time he drew abreast of the minicab the Jaguar was already turning the corner at the bottom of the slip road. He skidded to a halt.

A grass bank rose to Charlie's right, hiding the motorway from view. The grass was scored with tyre marks from where the vehicles had jockeyed for position. A man's body lay at the foot of the bank. The man was swarthy, broad-shouldered, packed with muscle. There was a tiny bullet hole in his left cheek. Most of the back of his head was missing.

Charlie looked away and found the driver of the minicab staring at him with empty eyes. Running down the side of his face was a long, purple bruise. It looked like he'd been killed not by a bullet, but a door pillar. Either way, he was dead.

Leaving the bodies where they were, Charlie scrambled up the bank. From the top he had a view of the motorway through the veil of fog.

The northbound lane was empty: the Doncaster police had blocked the entire carriageway just short of the service exit. Drivers on the southbound side were rubbernecking, bunching up as the they tried to see why Robin Hood Services appeared to be on fire.

Suddenly, the Jaguar appeared from behind the grass bank. It flew off the end of the slip road and on to the motorway.

Charlie watched it arrow along a road as empty as a runway. In the facing lane, cars were slowing to marvel at the unusual sight. Within seconds, their quarry had vanished. Charlie flicked the safety back on, and cursed.

It was over. They'd failed. They could continue the chase, but how long would Milos keep Dunja alive? The thought was overwhelming, almost too much to bear.

He sat down on the grass, gasping. His lungs rattled with the smoke he'd inhaled. His left knee throbbed. All he could hear—apart from his own ragged breathing—was the crackle of flames. When he lifted his head, all he could see were strange lights stitched through cloying fog: the orange flutter of the fires; the yellow glowing saucers of the petrol station canopy; the distant blue pulse of the patrol cars. *Beam me up, Scotty,* he thought.

He waited for his breathing to grow steady again. Around him the world was oddly calm. *He* felt calm.

Then came the rush of footsteps, and a keen, familiar voice.

'Charlie—are you okay? Charlie!'

Alex was there in front of him, on her knees, joining him on the grass. She looked him up and down, checking for injuries. 'Did you take a hit? I saw you go down...'

'Good as new,' he said, managing a smile. 'No holes.'

'I just thought…'

She stood up, held out her hands and pulled him to his feet. Behind her, the flames still flickered.

'We need to get moving,' he said, blowing vapour into the mist, 'before the trail goes cold.'

'I discharged my weapon,' said Alex, as they hurried back to the BMW. 'Twice. I hate that.'

'I'm glad you did. You did the right thing.'

'I know.'

'Saved my neck, Alex.'

'You're welcome. I just hate all the bloody forms I'll have to fill in when we get back.'

'We'll worry about the paperwork later. Right now I've got a new car to catch.'

'"I"? What happened to "we"?'

They'd reached the BMW. Charlie leaned on the open door, lifted his leg with a grimace and rubbed his knee. His trousers were ripped. Typical. 'Time to split up, old girl,' he said. 'There're bodies to be searched here and the local boys will need some steering.'

Alex looked pensive. He knew she wasn't fond of corpses. Who was?

'All right. But watch yourself, Charlie. You know what you're like when I'm not holding your hand. And this Milos character's playing hardball.'

'Tell me something I don't know. Still, Dunja's no slouch. So far he's given our assassin quite a run for his money. I just hope his luck hasn't run out.'

'None of this is adding up. Too many players.'

'I know,' Charlie said. 'It looks like Milos has finally got his man. But if he wants Dunja dead why didn't he just shoot him there and then?'

'Maybe he's not out to kill him like we thought. Maybe it's something to do with that grudge, whatever it is. Who knows—we might get a ransom demand before the end of the day.'

Charlie gazed up into the sky. Miraculously, he saw a patch of brilliant blue. 'See if they'll scramble a chopper,' he said. 'It looks like the weather might be lifting at last.'

'Then you'd better get moving. The clearer it gets, the faster they'll go. Oh—and don't forget to fill her up!'

He hated to lose any more time, but Alex was right. He filled up the BMW while she went to the counter to sort out the bill. At the next pump was a black Audi. Just as he finished, a woman stood up from where she'd been crouching behind the car.

'Is it safe to come out now?' she asked. She smoothed out a startlingly short skirt.

'Perfectly safe, miss,' said Charlie. 'Uh, I'm afraid I'm in a hurry. My partner there will help you if you need it.'

As he revved the engine, Alex appeared at his window, blocking his view of the woman and her car. Her skirt, too. When he put the window down, Alex thrust her fist inside. They nudged knuckles.

'Keep your knickers clean,' he said.

'Inside and out. Oh, and Charlie?' she added as he craned his neck to look past her.

'Yeah?'

'She's not your type.'

The burning wrecks were blocking the slip road, and Charlie wasn't going to risk damaging the undercarriage of the BMW on the bank. He drove back to the northbound entrance ramp. The cavalry was fighting through the jammed traffic: two fire engines, several police cars and an ambulance. He sped past the twelve-year-old traffic cop and back on to the carriageway. The locals had done well clearing the road and there was plenty of room for him to execute a perfect handbrake turn.

The revs dropped as the BMW skidded round to face north again. It sat on the road, motor growling. Was Hazbi Dunja still alive? He had no way of knowing. All he could do was stay on the assassin's tail, keep moving, keep closing in.

He pushed the accelerator to the floor.

12

March 1st
15:03
Ryhill, nr Wakefield

THE FIRST thing Milos did—once Anton had driven the Jaguar out of the service station and back on to the A1—was turn up the heating. The second was to reach into the glove box. His battered fingers found an owner's manual, a small torch, a half-melted chocolate bar. He wolfed down the chocolate and went back to his search.

Finally, he found what he was looking for.

He snatched it up: a heavy object wrapped in cotton cloth. Unrolling the cloth, he dropped the contents in his lap.

It was a revolver. An American Smith & Wesson Victory Model. His father's gun—a souvenir from the war. A .38 six-shooter with sandblasted finish. He'd entrusted it to Anton two weeks previously, when they'd been planning the operation. Anton had got it into the UK, kept it safe. Kept it ready.

Milos closed his throbbing fingers around the wooden grip. Another piece had fallen into place.

His father had never told him where he'd got the Smith

& Wesson, but after his death Milos had made it his own. He'd kept it clean, fired it regularly. It was now over sixty years old. But for the nick on the fluted barrel, it looked brand new.

Guns were never his first choice. He hoped he wouldn't have to use this one. He had other things in mind for his prisoners. But, right now, it was exactly what he needed to keep them in their place.

Hazbi Dunja was sitting directly behind him. Turning in the Jaguar's passenger seat, he leaned past the headrest and aimed the revolver straight at his captive's face.

'That's quite an antique,' said Dunja, in Croatian.

Milos didn't reply, just sat there enjoying the prickling sensation as the chill gradually left his body. Enjoying the weight of the revolver, the sense that it knew why it was here.

Gradually the heat did its work. It took several minutes for Milos's teeth to stop chattering, several more for the ache in his fingers to begin to subside. He held his tongue while his body recovered. Dunja fell silent too— maybe the look in his captor's eye had told him everything he needed to know.

Milos spent the time studying his prisoners. Up close, Dunja looked old. Old and spent. Maybe politics didn't suit him like the military. What was it like to go from driving a tank to driving a desk? Wouldn't a man lose something along the way?

Especially a man like Hazbi Dunja.

Dunja sneezed, and Milos noticed how red his eyes were, just as they'd been on the Airbus. Sweat made fine beads on his high brow. The man had more than just a cold—he was running quite a temperature. Was this really the same barrel-chested tank commander who'd stormed into the house in Zrmanjagrad? Who'd seemed to fill the tiny front room, dwarfing even Milos's father with his presence? Who'd sent his men to the back of the house to stop the women—Milos's mother, his two sisters—from escaping?

Who had given those dreadful orders?

For an instant, Milos wondered.

Then the car jolted, knocking Dunja sideways against the woman. Anger contorted his face, and in that instant Milos saw again the man he hated, the man he'd come all this way—and waited all these years—to kill. He wasn't weak at all, only ill. If not for the fever, he'd have been much less easy to abduct.

Fate was on Milos' side.

He turned his attention to the woman in the seat behind Anton. Where Dunja slumped, she sat erect. When Milos ran his gaze across her tanned face, her well-toned body, she looked right back at him, challenging him to make a move. Was she defiant or merely proud? He couldn't tell. It didn't matter. She was his—an attractive and unexpected bonus.

He almost hoped she would put up a fight. Beating her down might be almost as rewarding as what he had planned for Dunja.

As his fingers came back to life, Milos swapped the revolver from one hand to the other. He sucked the blood from his tattered knuckles, his grazed palms. His gaze never left the woman. Strange, to have his enemy in his grasp, yet to have eyes only for her.

'Who are you?' he said to the woman. He'd decided to speak Croatian too, just to keep them guessing. Dunja jumped, as if Milos had slapped him. Milos considered striking the gun barrel across his head, to reward him for his nerves. He decided against it. Time enough for that later.

The woman curled her lip and said nothing. Milos decided it would be a good idea to hit Dunja after all. He drew back the revolver. Again he saw the anger darken Dunja's face.

Still the animal inside. Perhaps this fever isn't as bad as you'd have me believe, Dunja. Are you just biding your time? Waiting for me to make a mistake?

He brought the gun down. Before it made contact, the woman's fingers were around his wrist, forcing it up against the ceiling. Milos felt Anton's arm move beside him, reaching for his own weapon.

He wrestled silently with the woman for two seconds, three… Surely Dunja would make his move now? But Dunja just watched with a strange expression on his face. Curiosity? From the driver's seat, he heard a metallic click. A glance confirmed Anton had drawn his Browning nine-millimetre.

At last, Milos wrenched his hand free. He pulled back the hammer and pointed the Smith & Wesson at the woman's chest. It wanted to shoot her—he could feel it. But he held it back. 'It's all right, Anton,' he said. 'Everything is under control. Just concentrate on your driving.'

The woman spat in his face. Milos let the spittle run down his cheek. When it reached his lips, he licked it off.

'Now you will tell me who you are,' he said, quietly. He used the gun barrel to nudge open the front of her coat, revealing the thin blouse underneath. 'If you don't, I will put bullets through both your lungs. You will then suffocate to death, in great pain. It seems a high price to pay for the sake of a name. Also, it will spoil the leather upholstery of this fine automobile.'

'Leave her alone,' said Dunja.

Without moving his gun hand, or his eyes, Milos said, 'If you speak again, I will shoot her anyway.'

Dunja leaned forward. Was the fool really going to call his bluff? He clenched his finger on the trigger.

With a sigh, Dunja sagged back in his seat.

The woman narrowed her dark eyes and said, 'Levnicki. My name is Jelenka Levnicki.'

'That's better,' said Milos. 'Now tell me—what special services do you provide for our esteemed Foreign Minister? You seem able to handle yourself but you don't look like a bodyguard.'

She glanced at Dunja. 'I'm a translator. What do you want from us?'

He raised the barrel of the revolver to stroke her cheek. She didn't flinch. 'A reasonable question. What I want first is to take you and your companion to a very safe place. Once we're there, I'll tell you everything you want to know. Now, in a moment I am going to turn my back on you. My neck is stiff—I must rest it. Before I do this I need you to be reassured neither of you are carrying any weapons.' He looked at Dunja. 'You first.'

'But how can I…?'

'Take off your jacket. Turn the pockets inside out. Do the same with your trouser pockets. I'll let you keep your trousers on, by the way.'

Dunja obeyed, spilling a wallet and a silk handkerchief into his lap. Transferring the gun to his right hand, Milos reached over the seat and ran his left hand quickly over Dunja's shirt, down his legs. Satisfied, he turned to the woman.

'Your turn.'

'Go fuck yourself!'

'When I've finished with you, perhaps I will. Now,

take off your coat. Perhaps you have a shoulder holster hidden under that pretty blouse.'

Glowering, she shrugged off the coat. Milos swapped hands again and frisked her. Her body stiffened as he felt for the holster he knew he wouldn't find. When he touched her breasts, she called him a bastard; when he stroked his hand down her thighs she called him a fucking bastard. It didn't stop him performing a thorough check.

'All right,' he said, when he'd finished. 'I'm going to turn round. Believe me when I say I can shoot you quicker than you can move. Do you doubt it?'

'No,' said Levnicki, pulling on her coat. Dunja said nothing.

Facing the front, Milos turned to Anton. 'Who was the man in the Range Rover?'

Anton shook his head. 'I don't know. My guess is British Secret Service.' His voice was brittle with anger. There was a dark splash of blood on the sleeve of his coat. Luka's blood. Like Dunja, he looked tired.

'That's what I thought.' Milos pondered this, uncertain. The Range Rover was unmarked—the man had to have been some kind of undercover agent. But working for whom? He'd been hungry for action, that was for sure. Almost too hungry…

If MI6 are on to me, perhaps it's time to go undercover. Time to go deep. They won't take kindly to me bringing old battles to their shores. They'll hunt me down, and they won't stop until they've found me.

He glanced in the wing mirror. Dunja stared back at him.

Not before I've dealt with you though.

His eyes were drawn back to the blood on Anton's sleeve.

'I'm sorry about Luka,' he said.

'Yes.' Anton bit off the word, as though he were afraid of saying any more.

'Was he carrying anything? Anything the police could use to identify him? Or us?'

'No papers,' said Anton. 'You know how we operate. Luka was clean.'

'Good.' Milos looked out of the window. Nothing but low hedges and weather-worn barns. 'So—where the hell are we?'

Twenty minutes had passed since they'd left the A1. As long as they stayed on the motorway, Anton had said, they were easy pickings. He was right. After the shoot-out at the service station, the police would be pulling out all the stops. And the fog had lifted at last. Clear skies meant helicopter surveillance. They'd have to work hard not to be tracked.

'Approaching Leeds,' said Anton. 'The mission's shot to pieces. This looks like the best way to salvage it.'

Milos nodded. The original plan had been to take Dunja to a deserted farm in Kent. Anton had found the location back in January. He'd left Luka camped there for a few days to make sure nobody was likely to visit. The farm was ideal for what Milos had in mind: quiet, secluded, no neighbours. Nobody to hear the screams.

Leeds wasn't ideal, but they'd used it before. Given how far north the chase had carried them, it was the logical alternative.

'You're sure the safe house isn't compromised?' Milos said.

'As sure as I can be. We'll approach with caution. At the first sign of trouble, we'll get clear. Don't worry. I've got contingencies.'

Milos nodded. Anton was good with contingencies.

'How far is it?' For the first time that day, Milos felt impatience building in him. He'd waited years for this, yes, and could wait a little longer. But Dunja was here, now. In his grasp. His fingers were tingling again, not with cold this time, but with rage. The revolver wanted to swing round and empty itself into Dunja's face. As for Milos himself: he wanted to finish it here and now, to rid himself of this burden, this debt to his family, this dreadful, all-consuming desire.

Oh, but what a waste that would be.

'If I go direct, we could be there in half an hour,' Anton was saying. 'But we have to stay on the back roads. We have to turn corners where they expect us to go straight. We have to keep our heads down.'

'Just get us there without being seen.'

The Jaguar followed the winding country roads. Progress felt slow now they'd abandoned the motorway. Then, through a gate across an open field, Milos saw tower blocks and chimneys. Moments later a sign turned them west towards Leeds. The traffic built as they approached one of the ridiculous mini-roundabouts the British seemed intent on constructing. Anton slowed the Jaguar to a crawl.

Out of the corner of his eye, Milos saw Levnicki's hand steal towards the rear door latch. He tilted his head, pretending to study the dashboard instruments. The woman's fingers closed round the latch. By now the Jaguar was doing little more than walking pace.

Levnicki's fingers clenched, pulled…and she threw herself against the door.

Nothing happened.

Shouting with rage, she hit the door again. Still it wouldn't open. She hammered the glass in frustration, then leaned across Dunja's lap, reaching for the other door.

'I wouldn't bother, my dear,' said Milos, without looking round. 'My friend here was smart enough to engage the child locks before setting off this morning. I think you'll also find the window mechanisms have been disabled.'

'You fucking pig!' shouted Levnicki, tossing herself back against the seat.

'Perhaps. But if you insist on drawing attention to yourself I will simply shoot you dead, here and now. As you may have guessed, my real interest in all this is the man you're sitting beside. So, much as it would pain me to deprive the world of such a wonderful physical specimen as yourself, I recommend you spend the rest of the journey sitting very, very still and shutting the fuck up!'

He turned to see a blush of anger flood up Levnicki's throat to her cheeks. She had more spirit than her boss, he had to give her that. After all these years, Hazbi Dunja was turning out to be a bit of a disappointment.

Realisation dawned on Milos.

Turning to face Dunja again, he said, 'You don't recognise me, do you?'

Dunja's lank hair had fallen across his brow. He pressed it back against his scalp and scowled at his captor. 'Should I?' he said.

'I don't know about "should",' Milos said. 'But you will. Believe me, before this day is out, you'll remember exactly who I am.'

13

March 1st
16:20
Cabinet Office, Whitehall

HENRY Worthington's hands shook as he lifted the carriage clock from the mantelpiece. Flipping open the small gilt door at the back, he wound it up. Eight turns. Any more and he'd wreck the mainspring. He closed the door, set the clock back in its place.

He straightened his back and checked his own internal mainspring. It felt ready to burst. Hands still shaking, he walked back to the window and watched the familiar Whitehall roofline appear out of the thinning mist. A flock of pigeons flew from shadow into late sunlight. They cast long, fluttering shapes through the gloom. The afternoon was coming to an end; somehow it felt like the day had only just begun.

Hazbi Dunja still hadn't been found. That was bad for everyone, but the longer the situation remained unresolved the worse it got for the department. And for Henry in particular. He was, after all, the one who'd sanctioned the visit in the first place. His testicles were still aching

after his meeting with Oliver Fleet and the Permanent
Secretary.

But blame, like an arrow, wanted nothing more than
to be aimed at a target. And Henry knew exactly what he
had to do to hit the gold. He returned to his desk and
opened his laptop, watched the screensaver for a moment, then launched the email programme.

The meeting with Burfield and Luard had ended in a
scrappy fashion. So much for being the ringmaster. As
soon as Burfield had told them what he knew about the
shoot-out at the service station—which at that stage was
very little—he had made his apologies and returned to
Scotland Yard. Luard had lingered for a while, clearly
eager to ingratiate himself with Henry. Henry knew what
that was all about: Luard just wanted to make sure MI6
was in the clear.

'I'm rather afraid,' Luard said, as soon as Burfield had
left, 'our friends in the Met have taken their eye off the ball.'

'Perhaps,' said Henry. 'But you're the ones who
dropped it in the first place.'

Luard flinched. 'My intelligence said that Milos was
a threat,' he said. 'You can't hold MI6 responsible for police bungling.'

'Leave the apportionment of blame to the experts,' said
Henry, 'and concentrate on what you do best.' He leaned
back in his chair, twirling a silver pen between his fingers.
'And it might do you good to remember whose office we
both must report to. Does "Security and Intelligence
Coordinator" mean anything to you? The clue's in the title,
by the way.'

'I don't need a lesson in…'

'I think perhaps you do, Nick. "Coordination" means
working together, MI6 and SOD. You and Brian Burfield,

if you prefer. If the two of you didn't spend all your time locking horns, we wouldn't have these undesirables running amok.'

'I think "running amok" is a bit strong…'

'Do you? A known assassin has kidnapped a high profile foreign official on British soil. Sounds like a grade one cock-up to me. Nick, if you know anything more about this than you're letting on, now's the time to tell me. If you don't, then get the hell out of my office and start co-operating with Burfield. We are all on the same side, you know.'

Luard stood. 'I'll help where I can,' he said. His face looked pinched, as if he'd smelt something bad. 'But the minute Dunja set foot on British soil this ceased to be my problem. If it's UK intelligence you're chasing, you should be talking to MI5. I've got the rest of the world to worry about.'

'Just get out, Nick.'

Even before Luard had left, the phone was ringing again. Henry waited until the door was closed before picking it up.

'Worthington.'

'Jack again, Henry. I've been hearing some nasty reports from up north. Shots fired, people killed. Sounds like the OK Corral. Plenty there to interest an old news hound like me and, well, you know what I'm like—I can't help putting two and two together.'

'And making five, as usual.'

'Maybe, maybe not. Just answer me this, Henry: is there any connection between the Doncaster shoot-out and your missing diplomat?'

You might be irritating, and I might rue the day you married my sister, and I might especially hate the way you drink my best Claret by the crate, but by God, Jack McClintock, you're sharp.

'Any connection...' he began, before stopping himself short. Jack was so crafty he'd almost got Henry to admit Dunja *was* indeed missing. Rumours were flying, of course, but his office had yet to make an official statement. 'You have an over-active imagination, Jack,' he said. 'Now, why don't you find yourself a real story?'

He had slammed down the phone.

Damage limitation. That's what matters now. Nick Luard's right about one thing: there was a bigger picture.

Time to put the events of the day in perspective. Yes, Dunja had missed today's meetings. But they'd just been the warm-up—a kind of diplomatic B-movie. The main feature wasn't scheduled until tomorrow: Dunja's address to the Scottish Parliament. If they found him in the next couple of hours, could they still get this back on track?

It didn't look likely. Even if Dunja turned up there'd have to be police interviews, a lengthy debrief—not least with the Prime Minister—and any amount of dialogue with Zagreb. By the time everything was smoothed out it would be too late to get Dunja up to Holyrood. Always assuming he was in a fit state to fly, let alone stand up and speak. No, it was looking more and more as if the entire trip was a write-off.

Of course, it could be worse even than that. Dunja could be dead.

The thought turned Henry's blood to ice. At forty-nine, he was old enough to smell the hot latte of retirement. The ultimate stimulant, these days it drove his every move. That and the knowledge that, if he kept his nose clean, he'd be able to drink that latte while admiring a shiny new OBE. All he needed on top was a brace of non-executive directorships to keep the wolves from the door.

At the same time, he had enough years left in office to make the most almighty foul-ups. Starting—and just possibly ending—with this one.

But when it came to self-protection, Nick Luard and Brian Burfield were amateurs.

Time for the master to go to work.

The first email he composed was to Luard. He began by reiterating what he'd said just before Luard had left: that MI6 were bound to co-operate with SOD at all times and on all levels. He made it clear that he considered Luard's department directly responsible for the entry of Javor Milos into the country.

> 'The failure of MI6,' he wrote, 'to anticipate the arrival on British soil of a known assassin can at best be described as careless. Some might actually consider it incompetent. Let us hope that Hazbi Dunja is found safe and well before this assassin succeeds in his mission. If not, serious questions will have to asked about the future administration of the Security Services.'

He sent a similar email to Burfield. This time he riffed on the initial failure of SOD officers to intercept Dunja at Stansted.

> 'Subsequently,' he added, 'you have allowed Hazbi Dunja to travel half-way up the country before being abducted at gunpoint by the very man you were supposed to be protecting him from. This failure of SOD to fulfil its primary function

is worrying to say the least, and suggests that a full
departmental review may be in order.'

When both emails were encrypted and sent, Henry felt a
little better. It did no harm to mark cards. And it was good,
actually, that Burfield and Luard scrapped as much as
they did. The dust they kicked up in the ring might stop
suspicious eyes turning in Henry's direction.

He poured himself a whisky and watched the hands
of the clock sweep round. Outside, it was beginning to
get dark.

He might yet come out of this unscathed.

14

March 1st
17:31
Royal Armouries, Leeds

AFTER nearly an hour cruising the outskirts of Leeds, Charlie finally admitted to himself that the trail had gone cold. He circled for a while longer, stomach knotted with frustration, before finally pulling the BMW into a lay-by near the river. He turned off the engine. The silence only seemed to amplify his anxiety. His whole body was aching from the long drive, not to mention the action at the service station; he even fancied his ears were still ringing from the gunfire.

He picked at the place where his trousers were torn. The red skin of his grazed knee peeked through the flaps of fabric. *Just like a kid in a playground.*

On the other side of the river rose the huge Royal Armouries building. The sky behind the museum was washed with purple dusk. Between the lifting of the fog and the onset of evening there had been a brief spell of late but brilliant sunshine. The flyboys had finally got their chopper off the ground and actually spotted the

Jaguar from the air, heading in towards the city along back roads. Charlie had kept pace, working with the Leeds traffic cops to construct a net in which they might catch their quarry.

Then—yet again—he'd been let down by a dodgy camera lens.

As the light failed, the helicopter crew had switched to the thermal imager…only to find a malfunction in the software that completely blanked the picture on their screens. By the time they'd rebooted the system, they'd lost the Jaguar.

'Whoever's driving knows the area,' they told Charlie when they relayed the bad news. 'He's sticking to the speed limits, making confident turns—not drawing attention to himself. At this time of night it's going to be hard to pick him up again.'

Charlie knew what they meant. It was rush hour and the roads were clogged up. There was no point just cruising aimlessly. Without any firm sightings, all he could do was sit and wait. He had a hunch Javor Milos wasn't far away. Why would he risk getting caught in city traffic unless there was somewhere in Leeds he needed to be?

His mind went back to the service station, to the man he'd glimpsed for just a second, rising up like a ghost between the silver Jaguar and the wrecked minicab…

Where are you hiding, Milos? And what's on your mind?

Charlie watched as the purple of the sky deepened to indigo. He felt tense and tired. Ironically, this was exactly how he'd felt last time he'd been here. That had been two years ago.

He'd brought his girlfriend Kathy to the Royal Armouries as a treat for her birthday. They'd spent the day walking through the huge museum halls. Charlie had marvelled at the ancient weaponry, the fabulous battle-dress. Kathy had spent the day grumbling that he'd brought her on a boy's own adventure.

'They used to have a lot of this gear on show in the Tower of London,' he said, as they climbed through an enormous stairwell. On the walls, rising four storeys, were what looked like ten thousand spears.

'It's a shame they didn't leave it all there.'

When they'd gone to the coffee shop for lunch, he'd tried to salvage something from the day. 'I'm sorry,' he said. 'I really thought you'd enjoy it. Aren't all teachers into history?'

Kathy held his hand across the table and told him, no, *she* was sorry. 'I know you've been trying hard, Charlie. And I do appreciate you bringing me up to Leeds. It's been tough lately, what with your shifts all over the place. And I know I get crabby when we're coming up to the end of the school term.'

'At least you get those long holidays to relax.'

She gave him that teacherly 'Don't even go there' glare.

'Charlie, we've been together six years now. In all that time we've had two holidays. Proper holidays, I mean. And today's the first time we've been anywhere—outside London I mean—all year.'

'I know. I'm sorry. But you said it yourself, my shifts…'

'Yes. Your shifts.'

The afternoon had gone better than the morning. There was a mock joust in the museum grounds and Charlie got them centre seats. They ate ice-cream and watched men who should have known better slice melons in half and knock each other off puzzled-looking horses. The sun shone and they laughed a lot.

Afterwards, in the car on the way back to London, Kathy told him it was over.

'Six years I've loved you, Charlie Paddon,' she said, 'and I know you've loved me. I think you still do. But you know what? I think you love your job just a little bit more.'

Charlie never gave her the souvenir he'd bought in the gift shop: a miniature silver replica of the horned Henry VIII mask that, at the time, the Royal Armouries had used for its logo.

'Good job you didn't,' Alex had said, when he'd told her the grim details the following evening. They were in the pub, taking the edge off after a long shift. The rest of the team had gone home. Charlie—uncharacteristically—had stayed for one more drink.

'Didn't what?' he said, brooding into his bitter.

'Give her this.' Alex turned the little silver mask over in her fingers.

'Why?'

'She's a girl, Charlie. What she really wanted was a ring.'

It was getting cold inside the BMW. Charlie ran the engine for a while. Save the planet, yes—freeze your balls off, no thanks.

His phone rang. He took the call and heard a familiar voice.

'Charlie—where are you?'

'Hi, Alex. Knocking back tequila in a Yorkshire lap-dancing bar.'

'They don't have lap-dancers in Yorkshire. Just sheep. If I know you, you're still trying to get the seat right in that damn BMW of yours.'

'Guilty, m'lud. What's new?'

'I'm still at the station in Doncaster. It's pretty grim,

Charlie. We've got three body bags and they're all occupied.'

'Three? Jesus!'

'Told you it was grim.'

'Who are they?'

'First up is the man from the Jaguar. You know—the one who got JFK'd.'

'Well, we knew he was a goner.'

'Yes. We're pretty sure he was working with Milos. No ID but I've asked Brian to run his description against Milos's known accomplices. I wouldn't be surprised if we get a match. Uh, second is a bit more of a puzzle. That's our mystery rifleman—the man who was driving the Range Rover.'

'He didn't make it, either?'

'He survived the explosion but he got burned pretty badly. Died an hour after reaching the hospital.'

'Who's the third?'

'The driver of the minicab. Shot three times, banged his head on the door jamb and bled to death with his meter still running. Like you said, he'd racked up one hell of a fare.'

She was trying to keep her report both light and professional, but Charlie could hear the tremor in her voice. The shoot-out had shaken her up—hell, he didn't feel so good himself. He was no stranger to fatalities, but three in one day…that was shocking.

'So as far as we know Dunja's still alive?' he said.

'That's the good news. The bad news is: so is Milos.'

'The way our luck's gone today, why am I not surprised? Alex—are you okay?'

'I'm fine.' Her voice had settled. Like him, Alex was dealing with the shit by concentrating on procedure. It was what you did. 'Uh, we've made some progress with the guy in the Range Rover. You know how we thought at first he might be one of ours? MI5, you said. Well, that was a nice try but no cigar—he wasn't. From the look of him he's from somewhere in Eastern Europe. Plus he's got tattoos on both arms written in some kind of Slavic language. Brian's checking to see if he's known to MI6. You never know—he could be connected to Milos somehow.'

'If so, why was he shooting at him?'

'Charlie, he was shooting at *you*.'

'Mmm.'

'Well, anyway, Brian's going to have a word with Nick Luard, see if he can give us any clues.'

'Better not hold our breath then.'

'Naughty, naughty, Charlie. People have been thrown in the Tower for less.'

Charlie's stomach growled. He sometimes wished he could keep going without having to stop for inconveniences like food and sleep. He wondered where he would find the nearest takeaway. 'Anything else?'

'Just hardware from the scene. The man who got shot in the head was carrying a handgun. There was another pistol lying on the ground under the minicab. Someone dropped it, don't know who. Forensics are trying for prints.'

'What kind of pistol?'

'A battered twenty-two—serial numbers filed off. Plenty of those on the black market.'

'All right. Keep going.'

'The dead man from the Jaguar was also carrying a mobile phone. Cheap pay-as-you-go Nokia, probably bought at a supermarket. The techies are trying to trace its call history.'

'Now that could be a good lead,' said Charlie. 'You're right: he must have been working with Milos. There's a good chance he used the phone to call up his boss, maybe even to arrange the rendezvous at the service station. If so, we might get a fix on a radio mast. At least that'll give us somewhere to start looking. The rifleman though... he's still a puzzle.'

'Roger that. Anything else on your mind?'

Charlie gazed at the hulking museum building. 'Just ancient history,' he said.

'Say again?'

'Uh, no, nothing from this end, Alex. Nothing you haven't heard a hundred times already, anyway. Keep me posted. I'm going to find something to eat. Over and out.'

Charlie felt in his pocket, pulled out the little silver mask of Henry VIII. He'd found it at the back of a drawer a couple of weeks ago and started carrying it around. He had no idea why.

Behind the city skyline, the moon was rising. It was huge, like an optical illusion. There was a reason for that, Charlie thought—something to do with the atmosphere. He was damned if he could remember what it was.

He dropped the mask back in his pocket, put the BMW in gear and slipped out into the traffic. In his rear-view mirror, the Royal Armouries grew smaller, and disappeared.

15

March 1st
19:13
Belle Isle, Leeds

ONCE they were out of the traffic and cruising the side streets, Milos drew his gun again. Dunja must surely sense they were close to their destination; if he was going to try anything, the time was now. Milos held the gun in his left hand and kept it low—no sense in advertising his trade.

'Where are you taking us?' said Dunja. He seemed more alert. The woman, Levnicki, sat beside him, silent and sullen.

'You'll find out soon enough,' Milos replied.

'It seems to me we have met before. Where was it?'

He didn't like Dunja asking him questions. *He who questions, controls.* With the gun in his left hand, he reached round the seat and pressed the barrel against his captive's knee. 'I can shoot your kneecaps without killing you. But it will be painful and messy. For your own sake, I suggest you be quiet!'

A half-smile formed on Dunja's face. He'd rattled his captor and he knew it. Milos pressed down the rage as it rose up into his throat. To distract himself, he glared through the window.

A road sign told him they were entering an area of Leeds called Belle Isle. Anton drove the Jaguar past a sprawling park, through a colourless gulag of social housing, finally down a series of wide, tree-lined avenues. Victorian red-brick houses slumped in shadow at the ends of long front gardens. Once they'd have been well-to-do; now many were flagged with student accommodation signs.

Belle Isle. As Anton turned the Jaguar into the drive of one of these old semi-detached hulks, he thought that whoever came up with such an exotic name had clearly never visited the place.

Milos remembered thinking the same thing last time he'd been here. It had been four years ago. His target had been another former member of the Croatian army, but without Hazbi Dunja's high profile. A professional hit for a client who'd preferred to remain anonymous. The job had been well-paid, free of emotion.

The assassination had gone without a hitch: a dark night and a stiletto, and the victim dropped silently into the lower reaches of the Thames. He and Anton had shared the driving up the motorway, using almost the same route they'd followed today. They'd spent the night in Leeds before travelling across to Manchester airport, from where they'd left the country. Everything sharp and clean, just like the knife he'd used to slit his target's throat.

What a contrast to today's disastrous chain of events.

But now he was here, the old Victorian safe-house made Milos feel, well, safe. Night had fallen, they'd lost the cops. Despite everything that had gone wrong, despite losing Luka at the service station, the predator had caught his prey.

All that remained was to decide exactly how to deliver the final blow.

Belle Isle. He opened the door of the Jaguar and breathed in the cold night air. What a charmingly ironic name for a killing ground.

Two big apple trees shielded the front of the house from the road. The house itself looked in poor repair; the adjoining semi was boarded up, apparently deserted. A rickety carport ran down the side of the house. Beneath it was another vehicle, draped in a black PVC cover. It was dark and the road was free of traffic. He checked the neighbouring houses and saw only closed curtains, back-lit blue with the flicker of television screens.

While Anton unlocked the front door, Milos stood on the gravel drive, flexing his back and puffing vapour up towards the stars. He kept his gun levelled at the Jaguar, just in case Dunja or the woman tried to scramble out through the front. Neither prisoner moved.

Anton made a couple more trips up the drive, ferrying bags from the Jaguar's boot. Eventually he returned, with his own gun drawn. Milos stepped back, let him open the nearside passenger door. Dunja shivered as the cold air wafted inside.

'Get out.' When Dunja didn't move, Milos pointed his gun once more at his knee and raised his voice. 'Now.'

Moving like an old man, Dunja clambered out. Even before he was upright, Anton had pulled a pair of hand-cuffs from his coat and snapped the first bracelet around his left wrist.

'Your other hand,' Anton said. 'Give it to me!' He wasn't interested in knees; instead he rammed his pistol into Dunja's cheek. 'Now tell me what you see on the back of this fine automobile.'

Using the gun, he pressed Dunja's face down towards
the Jaguar's boot. Half the rear bumper was splashed
with a dark, sticky substance.

'Blood,' said Dunja.

'Wrong,' said Anton. 'What you see is brains. The
man those brains belonged to was called Luka. He was
my cousin. If you don't want *your* brains to suffer the
same fate, I suggest you do exactly as I say!'

Dunja reached his right hand behind his back. Anton
closed the other bracelet, grabbed the chain and frog-
marched Dunja up the drive and into the house.

From the Jaguar's back seat, Jelenka Levnicki glared
at Milos.

'Your turn,' he said, smiling in the starlight. 'If you be-
have yourself, I promise not to use the cuffs.'

Even with his father's revolver pressed hard into her
back, he half-expected her to jump him as he walked her
inside. But she didn't. Perhaps she was concerned about
jeopardising her boss's safety. Or perhaps she just wasn't
as tough as she liked to appear. Milos guided her over the
cracked tiles of the porch and into the shabby hall. A
naked bulb glowed weakly halfway down, catching the
strands of old cobweb in the corners of the ceiling. When
they were both inside, he kicked the front door shut. The
latch closed with a soft click.

Anton reappeared, without Dunja. His face was
drawn. He was carrying a coiled nylon rope. Milos raised
his eyebrows.

'He's in the kitchen,' said Anton. 'Don't worry—he's
not going anywhere. Where do you want her?'

'The front room,' said Milos. 'Come with me, just in
case she gets clever.'

Like the hall, the front room smelled of mildew and

rot. Paper sagged from the walls; the carpet was thread-bare, the plaster coving cracked. *Once this room would have been grand,* Milos thought. *What a waste.* On the other hand, the squalor made it perfect for what he had in mind. Who was there to complain if he got blood on the carpet?

'Take off your coat,' he said to the woman. She did so, her eyes never leaving his. Milos grabbed the coat, tossed it into the corner of the room. 'Now kneel down.'

Levnicki hesitated. 'This carpet's crawling,' she said.

'Do as he says!' snapped Anton, stepping forward and waving his gun in her face.

'Steady,' murmured Milos. Like Anton, he was tired. But that was no excuse for mistakes.

Red with rage, the woman obeyed.

While Milos covered her with his revolver, Anton noosed her wrists behind her back and tied the rope around her waist. He contrived to pull at her blouse, hard enough to pop several buttons free. The blouse opened, revealing the tops of her breasts and the white lace of her bra. She was breathing hard. The dim light from the room's bare bulb glanced off the necklace she wore—a strange blend of leather and gem. As she fought for breath, the necklace jostled in her cleavage.

'Don't forget her legs,' said Milos, captivated by the necklace, and in particular by the valley of soft flesh it was nestling in.

'What do you think I am?' said Anton.

By the time he'd finished, Levnicki was on her side with her legs and ankles bound, and the rest of the rope tight about her waist. Her chest was thrust out in defiance. Her whole body looked stressed and taut. Again, Milos marvelled at what fine shape she was in.

A perfect dessert.

Once she was tied up, Anton flopped back on the sofa. He pressed his knuckles into his eyes.

'My head is aching,' he said. 'Too long on the road. And Luka …'

'Watch her,' said Milos. 'I'll be back. And don't fall asleep.'

The back of the house was in an even worse state than the front. The kitchen ceiling drooped; the red floor tiles—which must once have looked spectacular—were broken and grimy. The walls were black with mould.

In the middle of the kitchen floor, tied to a wooden chair, sat the Croatian Foreign Minister, Hazbi Dunja. Anton had stuffed Dunja's own silk handkerchief into his mouth and secured it with parcel tape. A small triangle of silk stuck out over his chin. On it, in gold thread, were the initials HD.

On the worktop beside the sink was one of the bags Anton had brought in from the car. Dunja watched, eyes wide, as Milos unzipped it. Metal chinked against metal.

From inside the bag Milos drew first a claw hammer, then a small hacksaw. Next came several pairs of pliers and a bradawl. One at a time, he set the tools on the worktop. As each tool emerged, Dunja's eyes bulged a little more. When Milos brought out the blowtorch, Dunja let out a whimper.

Milos sorted through the tools and eventually selected a Stanley knife. He unscrewed the two halves of the knife and plucked a new blade from its interior. He fitted the blade and screwed the handle back together. Scraping his thumb against the oil-coated steel, he turned to face his prisoner.

'Before I proceed,' he said, leaning back against the

worktop, 'I want to tell you a story. It's a war story. You do remember the war, don't you, Commandant?'

Perspiration was running freely down Dunja's face. Milos decided it wasn't just the fever making him sweat.

'Once upon a time,' he went on, 'in a small town called Zrmanjagrad, there lived a brave Serb called Marko Milos. When he was just eighteen years old, the Nazis invaded. Marko retreated into the mountains and fought with the Yugoslav resistance. He and his comrades lived in hidden caves and secret tunnels and shot as many Nazis as they could find. When the war eventually ended, Marko put away his souvenirs of battle and raised his family. Later—much later—another war started. Only this time it wasn't the Nazis who were the enemy.

'It was 1990 when things started getting really bad. Bad enough to make headlines around the world, at any rate. Even in America. When America notices you, you know things aren't going well. For five long years, an old and beautiful country was torn apart. Out in the world, nobody understood what was happening. They just heard the names: Serb, Croat, Bosnian, Kosovo... They didn't understand. It was just a bloody partisan war in a distant land they used to call Yugoslavia.

'But we understood. We all did. We knew what we were fighting for: independence. Not the independence born of treaty or debate, but of *heritage*. We were fighting to protect the soil our families had tilled for hundreds of years. That's what the rest of the world never understood: it was never about national borders. It was about the fences that ran outside our own front doors.'

Dunja was trying to shuffle the chair back across the kitchen, to little effect. Milos put down the knife and leaned close.

'I see understanding in your eyes, Hazbi Dunja. An animal you may be, but there is a part of you that knows what I know. That feels what I feel. We might have been brothers, in another life. You the dark half, I the light.'

He picked up the knife again, went back to stroking his thumb sideways across the blade. The rasping sound soothed him.

'By 1995, everyone knew the war could not go on forever. The Serbian forces were in poor shape, exhausted by their fight for freedom. In August, things came to a head. The Croatian army launched a major offensive. They bulldozed their way through Serbian territory. In doing so, they drove hundreds of thousands of Serbs out of their homeland. They called it Operation Thunder. The Serbs called it a crime against humanity. And some Serbs refused to leave. Marko Milos—along with his family— was one of them.'

Milos broke off. Something was thudding in the room. He realised it was his heart.

Bending down, he used the knife to slice a sliver of wood from the back of the chair. Unable to see what he was doing, Dunja writhed in panic. When he'd finished, Milos held up the splinter.

'The knife blade is sharp,' he said. 'There's a blade in this story. But I think you know that already, don't you?'

Dunja stopped struggling, just stared wide-eyed at his captor.

'It was just past noon. The sun was hot and the shadows were short. They came with tanks. The tanks rolled through the empty streets of Zrmanjagrad. The Croatian army wanted to drive the people from their homes, but the people had already fled. Everyone but Marko Milos and his wife, his daughters, and his son.

'It just so happened that the man in charge of the lead tank battalion—an ambitious young officer called Hazbi Dunja—stumbled upon the Milos house. Perhaps he saw wisps of smoke leaking from the chimney, even though the Milos girls had worked to damp the fire. Perhaps he saw the old motorbike leaning against the paddock wall and wondered who would leave such a treasure behind. It doesn't matter. All that matters is that he led his men up the drive and ordered them to encircle the house. Then he kicked down the door.

'Picture it. I know you can. Perhaps you dream of it still, as I do.

'There is the family, cowering in the small front room. Marko is coming down the stairs. He's carrying the old Winchester rifle his father brought back from America in 1920. It's the same rifle he used to shoot Hitler's Nazis and now he's levelling it at the face of the Croatian tank commander who has violated his home. He pulls the trigger, but the rifle misfires and the barrel explodes. It hasn't been fired for forty years, you see. Sometimes things just get old.

'The noise is deafening. Everyone in the room ducks or jumps, including the tank commander. Meanwhile, Marko has dropped the Winchester. One side of his face is black with soot. In the wall beside his head there is an enormous hole in the plaster. He draws his revolver—another souvenir from the United States. But he's forgotten to load it. It could almost be a comedy. Almost. So he draws his hunting knife.

'Marko hurls himself down the stairs, a grey-haired warrior with all his own teeth, and stabs at the Croatian tank commander. Dunja raises his hand to protect himself and the hunting knife chops the top off his index finger.

'Then Dunja's corporal uses his machine gun to cut Marko Milos in half.

'The women start screaming. The son starts screaming. The Croatians pour into the room through the front door, through the back. They smash the china, kick the furniture aside. Suddenly the small room is full of men. Dunja is clutching his injured hand, shouting orders. The son runs at Dunja, but two of the soldiers grab him and pin him to the floor. They force him to watch while they rape his mother and both his sisters. The son is old enough to have grown his first beard, young enough to howl like a wolf at what he is forced to witness.

'When the soldiers have finished, they use their bayonets to slit the women's throats.

'Then they turn to their commander and ask him what to do with the boy. "Let him go," says Dunja. "What better torture can we inflict?"

'So the boy runs into the woods behind the house. He hides there as the house slowly empties. Eventually, the tanks move on. They rumble down the street; the whole town reverberates to the sound of the metal treads.

'When all is quiet again he returns to the house. He goes to the back door but he cannot bring himself to go inside. He knows what he will see. Instead he stands in the mud, beside his father's wrecked motorbike, with his hands pressed against his cheeks. He stands there, feeling the soft down of his first beard thrusting back against his palms. He understands that he is alive. He has been left alive for a reason. It is this that gives him the strength to go back into the house.

'He closes his eyes as he moves through the rooms. His feet crunch on the broken china. He kicks something soft and bulky on the floor. It may be an overturned chair, or the body of his mother. He doesn't know. When he reaches the stairs, he drops to all fours. Step by step, he works his way up. On the fourth step he finds his father's revolver.

'Upstairs he finds the bullets his father forgot to put in the gun. He is about to leave when he thinks of one more thing he must have. It is in his bedroom. He goes to his room, takes it, and leaves the house. He never goes back.'

Leaning over, Milos touched his cheek against the side of Dunja's face.

'Do you feel how smooth it is?' he said. 'On that day in 1995, I vowed I would be clean-shaven again only when I had your life in the palm of my hand. Now that day has come.'

He stood back, appraised the fear in Dunja's eyes. Snot ran from the Croatian's nose, across the parcel tape holding the gag in his mouth. Milos's heart was hammering louder. This was like no assassination he had ever carried out before.

He looked down at Dunja's hands. They were gripping the arms of the chair, white-knuckled. He touched the knife blade to the clenched fingers, one at a time. With each touch, Dunja flinched. Milos ended with the blade resting lightly on the little finger of his prisoner's left hand.

'One by one,' he said, 'you cut my family from me, until only I remained. Now I repay the favour. I will cut *you* away, one piece at a time. Your fingers, your toes, your ears, your tongue, your eyes. The last thing I take will be your heart. It will still be beating when I cut it out of your chest.'

He tightened his grip on the knife and prepared to apply pressure.

Something buzzed against his chest. For a second, he thought it was his heart, bursting open at last.

But it was the mobile phone.

He almost laughed. The timing was extraordinary. But the smile never reached his face. Slowly, he drew the mobile from his inside pocket. The number on the display was Luka's.

Luka had been shot in the head.

He froze, staring at the phone. It continued to vibrate in his hand.

Could he still be alive?

Surely not. Even if he was, he'd be in a hospital ward—intensive care probably—with a police guard. But his head was blown apart!

It couldn't be Luka.

The phone stopped ringing. Dunja's eyes showed curiosity now, as well as fear. Keeping his grip on the knife, Milos dropped the mobile on the worktop.

'Wrong number,' he said, smiling with all his teeth. 'Now, where was I?'

The mobile started vibrating again.

This time it was the knife he dropped. As the phone danced its way across the dusty Formica, he snatched up the claw hammer and brought it down on the wretched device. The first time he missed—it was like trying to smash a rat. The second time he hit the mobile's LCD screen dead centre. The phone exploded into plastic shards and shreds of circuitry.

The kitchen was suddenly silent. Milos couldn't even hear the beating of his own heart.

They've got Luka's phone. If they're calling this number that means they can track us down, whether I answer it or not.

We've got to get out of here!

He snatched up the knife again, pressed it to Dunja's throat.

'I will not be cheated,' he hissed. 'Are you ready to die?'

16

THE BEST thing about the late shift, thought Henry, *is that Jack McClintock is less likely to call.*

Still, he eyed the phone with unease. You never could tell.

To his relief, there had been nothing in the *Evening Standard* about today's diplomatic crisis. He'd half expected to find a photograph of the Foreign Secretary on the front page, looking glum without his Croatian friend. There had been enough photographers hanging around. On a quiet news day, they might just have made a story of it.

Luckily, there was plenty going on in the House of Commons, what with the opposition getting all the mileage they could out of the latest data protection scandal. And the 'Battle of the Boy Bands' event at Wembley Arena ensured the centre pages were littered with celebrities. Thank heaven for C-list mercies.

Henry had spent most of the afternoon on the phone. He'd had to deliver hourly updates to Oliver Fleet (who had irritatingly started referring to the crisis as the Dunja

Debacle). That was tough, especially when there was so little to report. Henry was pleased, therefore, when Brian Burfield had called, saying he was on his way over.

'Have you got him?'

'Not yet. But we've got a positive lead.'

'What kind of lead?'

'I'll explain when I get there. Give me ten minutes.'

Henry had spent those ten minutes on what might (he later considered) have been the most critical telephone conversation of the day. Critical for his career, at least. A few seconds after Burfield had rung off, he'd received a call from the Scottish First Minister.

It wasn't the first time he'd spoken to Andrew Molloy. Molloy was a formidable politician and, Henry believed, a good man. For a national leader he was remarkably unassuming: a quiet thinker who had to speak only a few, measured words to reduce a room to silence. The media treated him with a reverence that was the envy of his rivals—and many of his colleagues. He was as much a nonstick merchant as Oliver Fleet, but with one critical difference: nobody threw mud at him in the first place.

Molloy's only fault—if it could be called a fault—was that he didn't suffer fools gladly. Unfortunately, he was also one of the few people Henry had ever encountered who made him feel like, well, a fool.

Molloy's opening salvo set the tone.

'Does Whitehall delight,' he said in his soft East-coast lilt, 'in throwing tomatoes every time Scotland appears on the world stage?'

Uncharacteristically flustered, Henry fumbled his way through a reply. Molloy cut him short.

'Scotland may be taking her first baby steps in international politics,' he said, 'but she's not quite as tottery as you may think. And as her stewards, we in the Parliament don't take kindly to being sabotaged by our so-called brothers-in-arms.'

'Please, Andrew, "sabotage" is putting it rather strongly,' said Henry. 'I can assure you…'

'Assure me that Hazbi Dunja is safely in police custody? I'd feel better if you could, Henry. But I don't think you can, can you? In fact, I rather doubt you can assure me he's even alive. The fact is, the Croatian Foreign Minister—who I might remind you is due to address the Scottish Parliament in just over twelve hours' time—is somewhere in England with a Serbian assassin on his tail. All because you failed to keep him in your care. Tomorrow was to be a big day for Scottish politics. And I can't imagine a bigger spanner than this going in the works. So I think "sabotage" comes pretty close to the mark, don't you?'

Throughout, Molloy's voice remained soft. Somehow, it was worse than if he had been shouting. Henry fumbled through his responses, listing the chain of 'unhappy accidents' and assuring Molloy that Whitehall was doing 'everything in its power' to bring the situation under control.

Being First Minister, Andrew Molloy made sure he had the last word.

'The only solution is to resolve the crisis. It's either that or go public. This needs dealing with, Henry. Tonight, please.'

Henry put down the phone feeling depressed. Throughout the conversation he'd been careful to refer to Whitehall in the third person, to distance himself from the issues. What was he but a public servant, simply doing his job? Henry Worthington, responsible for this crisis? How could anyone think such a thing!

But the fact remained that he was the one who'd got Dunja's visit—this whole diplomatic travelling show—on the road. Now, thanks to events entirely out of his control, it had driven itself right off a cliff. *He* was the one who ought to be feeling sabotaged.

He checked the clock. Where the hell was Burfield?

Sticking his head round the door, he found the SOD Chief Superintendent chatting to Eileen over a cup of coffee.

'Eileen said you were on an important call,' Burfield said. The top of his head barely came up to the chin of Henry's statuesque PA. It was like looking at an optical illusion.

'Brian,' said Henry. 'As soon as you are fully refreshed, why don't you come and join me?'

'Sarcasm isn't your style.'

'I've decided to adopt it. Any objections?'

Burfield followed him into the office. 'Your playground, your rules.'

Henry was about to close the door when he noticed Eileen staring at him. Her right eyebrow was raised in a familiar arch.

'Eileen,' he said, 'I'm sorry. Of course, you can go. I hope your evening hasn't been spoiled.'

'Don't worry, sir. I don't know the meaning of the word.'

'What—"spoiled"?'

'No, sir—"evening".'

The eyebrow stayed up but Henry fancied there was a trace of a smile on Eileen's lips. He watched her disappear down the corridor. The click of her heels blended into the sound of the floor buffer working its way in the opposite direction. In the distance he heard a door slam, someone shout, 'Goodnight!'

Brian was checking his watch against the carriage clock on the mantel.

'Two minutes slow,' he said as Henry closed the door.

'You or me?' Burfield just smiled. 'Look, Brian, before we start, I've decided to go public on this one. I'm going to officially cancel Hazbi Dunja's speech to the Scottish Parliament. I'll set the balls rolling on that this evening. By tomorrow morning, I'll have a press release ready to explain how the Croatian Foreign Minister was abducted by a foreign assassin, right from under our noses.' He crossed his arms and straightened his back. 'Actually, Brian, it was from under *your* nose, wasn't it?'

Brian drank the rest of his coffee and put the cup and saucer down on the meeting table.

'Will that be all right on there?' he said. 'Or will it spoil the varnish?'

'Sod the varnish! Haven't you got anything to say?'

'Actually, yes. That's why I came here, remember? To tell you about the lead we're following up?'

Henry stood for a moment more, then sank into his chair. He rubbed the back of his neck—it was stiff. Pain was beginning to shoot up into his skull. It had already been a long day, and he didn't imagine the night was going to be much better.

'All right,' he said. 'Tell me what you know.'

'As you know, we tracked them as far as Leeds before we lost them.' As he spoke, Burfield paced back and forth. His eyes were bright. 'Charlie Paddon's been there all evening; Alex Chappell's on her way to meet him again after finishing up in Doncaster.'

'Where the shooting occurred?'

'Yes. The Doncaster incident was where we got our break: a mobile phone. We think it belonged to one of

Javor Milos's accomplices. It was brand new, unregistered. Only one number on the recent calls list. We dialled the number twice. It rang both times, but nobody answered. After that we just got automatic voicemail.'

'Do you think the assassin has the other phone?'

'We're proceeding on that assumption. Now, because the phone actually rang the first couple of times, we can use phone masts to track the signal. That narrows things down significantly.'

'Not enough to pinpoint a location, surely?'

'No. But we do know the phone's within a ten-mile radius of a particular mast in south Leeds. Our friends at MI5 have given us a list of suspect properties in the vicinity. Places they've had their eye on. I have to say, they've been particularly helpful in that regard.'

Burfield looked straight at Henry when he said this. He was so transparent: he might as well have tacked the words 'unlike that bastard Nick Luard' on the end of his sentence.

'So what's the next step?' Henry said.

'Local police. Cross-referring MI5's data with the mast location gives us a shortlist of fifteen properties. I want them to go in and search them all. But I wanted to fill you in first. Bigger picture and all that.'

Was Burfield applying some sarcasm of his own? Henry couldn't be sure. 'How long will it take to do the searches?'

'Not as long as you might think. I think we'll know the house as soon as we see it. We know what we're doing.'

'Like you knew what you were doing this morning?'

Burfield looked genuinely pained at this. 'Shit happens, Henry. You know that. At least we're shovelling it up.'

Henry rubbed his eyes. He wondered if he'd actually manage to get any sleep tonight. On the plus side, the pain in his head wasn't getting any worse. Outside the office, the cleaners had reached Eileen's desk. The sound of the floor buffer was soothing.

'All right,' he said. 'You must do whatever you have to do, of course. But hear this, Brian, and hear it well. If you screw this up, we'll have a major international incident on our hands.'

For the first time that evening, Brian Burfield smiled. 'I thought we had one of those already.'

17

March 1st
20:05
Central Police Station, Leeds

ALEX ran up the police station steps, her body protesting all the way. It seemed as if the drive from Doncaster had taken forever. She was tired and thirsty and her backside was sore: the Zafira she'd borrowed from the Doncaster pool needed a suspension transplant. She wanted a hot cup of tea and a seat that didn't kick her arse every couple of seconds.

Charlie was waiting for her in the canteen, looking pretty good, considering. He sat up a little straighter, flashed her a grim smile and pointed at a big stainless steel teapot in the middle of the table. It was handy being partnered with a mind-reader.

'Boy, am I glad you're here,' he said as she threw herself in the chair opposite. He sounded tired, but still upbeat.

'Of course you are. You need me to solve the case for you, Sherlock.'

'I always thought of myself as more of a Jane Tennison.' Charlie poured the tea. 'Sorry there's nothing stronger.'

'You'd never get into the frocks.'

'You'd be surprised.'

She rubbed her eyes. 'Before we get too deeply into the cross-dressing, are you going to tell me what progress you've made?'

'I am. But first drink your tea.'

They chinked cups and she sipped the strong brew. Alex tried to get comfortable, but the chair was hard, the table tilted and the canteen badly lit, with two fluorescents out and a third flickering like crazy.

Alex had managed to get her bedtime call in to Fraser from the station at Doncaster. He'd been baking with Danni (Alex could only imagine the mess) and was high on stickiness and sugar. He'd giggled at her for a full minute before yawning and telling her it was time for her to 'go get baddies'.

After blowing him a kiss through the ether, she'd tried to call Lawrie in Aberdeen. She got bumped straight to his voicemail, so she left a message, told him she loved him and that Fraser was fine. He'd pick up the message if he remembered to switch his phone on. Her husband wasn't nearly as *au fait* with gadgets as their two-year-old son.

She finished her tea and poured herself another. Leaning back in the chair, she lifted both arms over her head and stretched until her spine popped. 'I never thought I'd say it, but I actually miss that pretty red BMW of yours. Vauxhalls just aren't the same.'

'I knew you'd come round, sooner or later.'

'So, come one then, tell me where we're at.'

Charlie stifled a yawn. 'The entire Leeds force is out searching houses. That's what it seems like, anyway. They tell me our diplomatic crisis is even more exciting than Saturday night at closing time. As for us—we just get to sit and wait for them to come up with something.'

'So what do we do in the meantime: spend the whole night drinking tea?'

As if to answer her question, the canteen door banged open. A stocky policeman crossed the room, bulldozing a chair aside in his haste to get to the table.

'DI Watts,' he said. He was red-faced, bright-eyed and looked like he played rugby at least seven times a week. 'Just came on shift half-an-hour ago. I was catching up with this mess of yours when the call came in.'

'What call?' said Charlie.

'We've just raided a house in Belle Isle. Looks like we've got something. A body.'

With Watts in the back seat of the BMW giving directions, it took them just ten minutes to reach the Leeds suburb. There was no mistaking the house: two patrol cars were parked at the front, lights flashing off the big trees concealing the drive from the road. A few neighbours huddled in porches, or peered through curtains, watching the excitement.

Alex followed Charlie through the gate. He hadn't spoken since they'd got the news about the body. Apparently it was messy. She was expecting to see the silver Jaguar but, to her surprise, the drive was empty. Down the side of the house was a carport. That was empty, too. But there were tyre-marks in the gravel, marks deep enough to have been made by a car leaving in a hurry.

'Did it rain here earlier?' asked Alex, bending to examine the tracks.

'A shower,' said Watts. 'After the fog cleared. What have you got?'

'Water in the ruts. These marks are fresh.'

Watts went to speak to the constable standing guard at the front door; the sentry was still supporting the Blackhawk ram he'd used to gain entry. Looking at the state of the rest of the house, Alex thought he could probably have opened the door just by breathing on it. But, as they put on the Scene-of-Crime overshoes and nitrile gloves Watts was dishing out, she noticed a brand new mortise lock and dead bolts on the inside. The place was in bad shape, but someone had gone to the trouble of making it secure.

'Body's in the front room,' said Watts. 'Go in. Forensics'll mutter when they get here, but you'll be wanting to see everything.'

'Yes, thanks,' said Alex. She felt the corners of her mouth turning down. She'd seen too many corpses today. One look at Charlie's grim expression told her he felt the same. To make matters worse, the dead man could only be Hazbi Dunja, the man they'd been assigned to protect.

She couldn't believe how the day had turned out. Twelve hours ago they'd been on their way to Heathrow Airport to meet the Croatian Foreign Minister off his plane. A big event but, fundamentally, a routine one. How had they come to find themselves here, halfway up the country, with a trail of dead bodies behind them? A trail that had led them here, to a grotty front room in south Leeds, where that same Foreign Minister had become a murder victim. And whose murderer had got clean away. The worst of it was, the day wasn't over yet.

Holding her breath, Alex stepped across the threshold and into the room.

The smell hit her first: that sharp, coppery blood-odour. It was something she'd never got used to. It was

a machine smell, the antithesis of life. Maybe that was
fitting, since it was the stench of death.

The dead man lay sprawled on a tatty sofa. His arms
and legs were splayed wide; his head was tipped back—
too far back. The ragged wound on his neck gaped wide.
Mercifully, the light was bad, so the interior of this ob-
scene second mouth was in shadow. Still, she saw something white glistening inside the gore. Bone. *Jesus, the
cut goes all the way through to his spine!*

The man's chest and shoulders, and the back of the
sofa, were black with blood. There was a spray of blood
on the wall behind him, released from his ruptured carotid
artery. Beside him, on the cushion, was a red-handled
Stanley knife. The blade looked tiny.

*You'd have to put your back into it, to make a cut that
big with a knife that small.*

Alex took a step closer, not wanting to look, but needing to see his face. Charlie moved with her. She was
holding her breath. She leaned over and prepared to make
the formal identification.

Beside her, Charlie did the same. Simultaneously, they
reached the same conclusion.

The man wasn't Hazbi Dunja.

While Charlie stepped away and started poring over the
rest of the room, Alex lingered beside the corpse. Relief that
this wasn't their man quickly gave way to concern as to who
else it could be. The owner of the house, perhaps, murdered
because he was in the wrong place at the wrong time?

Then she remembered the locks on the door. Milos and
his cronies had got this place ready in advance. If this man
was the owner, he was in on it, too.

She peered at the upturned face, imagined it animated,
alive. As soon as she did that, she recognised him.

'He was at the service station,' she said. Charlie, who had knelt to study a tangle of rope on the floor, looked up. 'He had a gun—he was firing at the Range Rover. I'm pretty sure he ended up behind the wheel of the Jaguar. I think we just found our getaway driver, Charlie.'

'You're sure?'

'Sure as eggs.'

Charlie continued to study the rope. Silently, he pointed out other things to Alex: a long scuff-mark in the grimy carpet; a discarded coat; a pair of women's shoes—black patent leather, low heels.

Alex heard a cough behind her. She whirled round, heart hammering. It was DI Watts, more-or-less filling the doorway.

'Sorry, Sergeant,' he said. 'Didn't mean to startle you.'

Charlie straightened up. 'This is it?' he said. 'Nobody else in the house?'

Watts shook his head. 'Not a soul, dead or alive. Small weapons cache upstairs. Some interesting items in the kitchen, too.'

'What could be more interesting than this?' said Alex.

To her relief, the kitchen was a blood-free zone. On the floor, there was an overturned chair; on the worktop an open tool bag. The tools were arranged like a surgeon's instruments. Seeing them laid out like that made Alex shiver. Beside the chair there was more rope and the shattered remains of what looked like a mobile phone. The back door was wide open, admitting a cold March breeze.

'Looks like someone didn't want to take our call,' said Charlie, pointing to the smashed phone.

'I'll leave you to it for a minute,' said Watts. 'I need forensics here now and they've only got two speeds: slow and stop.'

'Time for you to chivvy them along?' said Alex.

'Something like that.'

When Watts had gone, Charlie crossed the kitchen to the back door. He moved carefully, not touching anything, even with the gloves: this was a murder scene, after all. Alex continued to stare at the unsettling line of tools.

What the hell went on in here?

'What d'you think?' said Charlie, peering out into the garden.

'I don't know. I'm still trying to piece it together.'

Alex finally managed to tear her eyes from the worktop. She scanned the dusty floor, registering footprints, signs of a scuffle…

Charlie moved his foot. Light glinted off something lying beside the back door.

It was a pendant, leather, with crystals attached by twine. A curious mix of styles. *Catholic-ethnic*, she thought, *if there is such a thing*. Its thin leather strap was broken.

Charlie broke into her reverie. 'Come on, partner— let's think this through.'

'Okay—fire away.'

'Item one: we know Milos got into the Jaguar. You saw him as well as I did.'

Alex nodded. 'He must have crashed the bike,' she said, 'then crawled between the two cars for cover while the others were shooting it out. I only saw him when he stood up.'

'And you're sure the man in the front room was the one driving the Jaguar?'

'Yes. Which makes him Milos's accomplice. But then who was the man in the Range Rover, the one with the rifle?'

'I don't know. We won't know until they ID his body. Let's stick with what we've got here: Milos's driver lying in a pool of blood with his throat cut. Who killed him? Milos himself? Doesn't seem likely. Could it have been Dunja?'

Alex stared at the rope on the floor. It lay in several pieces, the ends cut clean.

'They had Dunja tied up,' she said slowly. 'Somehow he got free, managed to kill the driver, got out of the house…'

'So where is he now? Why is he so keen on running all the time? He's visiting Britain to make a speech, for God's sake. Why hasn't he called us? And where the hell is Milos?'

Alex could feel Charlie's anger like a pulse in the air. It was infectious; she had to fight to keep a lid on her own frustration. *Clear head*, she told herself. *It's the only way you'll think straight.*

Her eyes returned to the pendant. 'Don't forget the translator,' she said. 'I assume the shoes and coat in the front room are hers. Unless Milos had a female accomplice, too. I just don't know…'

Charlie ran his hands through his hair. Under the harsh glare of the light he looked pale and more tired than ever. It had been a long day. Nor did it look to be ending any time soon. He closed his eyes, tipped his head back.

'What's going on here?' he said. 'We're running out of time.'

Watts returned. 'Forensics say they'll be five minutes. Course, they said that ten minutes ago. Thought you'd like to know: we've been doing door-to-doors. An old codger who lives over the road confirmed four people arrived in a silver Jag. But—here's the thing—he only saw two leave.'

'In the same vehicle?' said Charlie.

'In the Jag. He saw it pull out of the drive in a real hurry, came downstairs to get a better look. By the time he'd found his keys and got the door open, they were gone.'

'But he saw two people inside?'

'Yes.'

'Male or female?'

'Unknown.'

Alex stared at Charlie. 'That still leaves one person unaccounted for,' she said.

'But which one?' Edging his way past the fallen chair and its array of evidence, Charlie joined her at the kitchen door. 'Come on, let's get some fresh air.'

Outside, they stood side by side, staring up at the front of the big Victorian semi.

'These were grand old places once,' Charlie said. 'Shame to see them go to rack and ruin like this.'

'Shame to have murders committed in their front rooms.'

'I don't know. I'll bet all these old houses have seen their share. You know what they say about the suburbs.' He exhaled. Vapour billowed out into the cold air. For some reason, Alex found her mind returning to the pendant. It was a curiosity: somehow both crude and classical.

'I have a hunch,' Charlie said, 'and it's only a hunch— that the two people in the Jag were Dunja and his translator. Somehow they escaped from Milos. And you know what? I think Dunja's trying to get to Scotland. Tonight.'

'But why not just turn himself in?'

'Alex, he's spent the whole day not turning himself in. Why start now? I think it's time we stop thinking of Hazbi Dunja as a stuffed-shirt diplomat and remember what he really is: an ex-officer of the Croatian army with more combat experience that we've had hot dinners. Maybe he trusts himself more than he trusts us.'

'That's quite a hunch.' But she had to admit it felt plausible. 'If you're right, it's Milos we're missing. Where is he?'

'I don't know. But given what we know about the man—and what we've seen today—I'm guessing he's not out of the picture yet. The point is, without any evidence to the contrary, we have to assume Hazbi Dunja is still alive. And I reckon he's planning to keep his appointment at the Scottish Parliament tomorrow. Which means you need to go to Holyrood. Right now.'

Alex peeled off the gloves and stuffed her hands in her pockets. 'Edinburgh?' she said. 'Tonight?'

'Yes. I really think Dunja's going to be there. I think that's what this whole crazy chase up the country has been all about. And if that's the case, SOD has to be there to look after him, as ordered. Especially if Javor Milos is still on the loose.'

'Seems to me Hazbi Dunja can look after himself.'

'I'd feel better if you were at Holyrood.'

'Can't wait to get rid of me?'

'You're expected to be there, Alex.'

'But there's a corpse in that house.' She fought to keep the bitterness out of her voice. 'You need me. You know I'm good with corpses.'

'Alex.' He put his hand on her shoulder. 'Do I have to pull rank?'

She shrugged him away. 'You just want me to spend another six hours in that bloody Zafira. Oh, and by the way—what *do* they say about the suburbs?'

Charlie looked up at the house. 'It's where all the bodies are buried.'

18

March 1ˢᵗ
22:21
A1, Berwick-upon-Tweed

THE SCOTTISH border was close. He gunned the engine and felt the car leap forward in response. Ahead, in the moonlight, the River Tweed was as sharp as a scalpel blade. Just as sharp were the red tail lights of his quarry. They danced before him, just as they'd danced all the way from Leeds. Taunting him. For perhaps the twentieth time, he slammed the heel of his hand against the dashboard and cursed.

I should have killed him when I had the chance!

He'd wanted to. It would have been so easy. Instead of smashing the mobile he should have smashed Dunja. Cut his throat there and then. Got it over with, got out of the house, out of the country. Gone to ground at last. This was, after all, the perfect time to consider retirement. With Dunja dead, his life's work would be complete.

But that was the thing: this *was* his life's work. It had to be done right. Revenge had to be served cold.

He'd held the knife blade against Dunja's neck for ten

long seconds before finally jerking it away. Dunja had cried out, perhaps convinced the sudden movement meant his throat really was cut. Milos had put the knife down and grabbed a crowbar out of the tool bag. Seeing Dunja flinch, Milos once more considered ending this now, dispensing with the torture and running.

Instead, he'd rushed upstairs. Dunja would keep. Right now, his priority was relocation.

They were compromised, badly. The phone call meant the police had Luka's body. The call they'd placed meant they were running a trace. It was only a matter of time.

Damn them!

He burst into the back bedroom. A streetlight made hard shadows on the peeling plaster wall. On the bed, framed in a square of light from the window, was one of the bags Anton had brought in from the Jaguar.

He dropped the crowbar beside the bag and started hauling the wardrobe across the floor. The wardrobe was solid oak. Moving it took both effort and precious minutes. It also made a lot of noise. The noise was something he later came to regret.

How long before the police turned up? Enough time to get out? He thought so. However good their trace was, it would only get them as far as the nearest phone mast. Which left a lot of ground to search before they pinpointed the house.

But people saw things, and neighbours got suspicious, however careful you were.

Best to assume they were already on their way.

With the wardrobe pushed aside, he knelt and pulled back the carpet. It rolled easily: it wasn't long since it had last been moved. He snatched the crowbar off the bed and used it to lever up the floorboards. The wood splintered but there was no need for care. This house was no longer safe; they wouldn't be using it again.

Under the floor was a hessian sack. He hauled it out, turned its contents out on to the bed.

There were two Heckler & Koch automatic rifles, one with a telescopic sight. Six boxes of 7.62mm bullets for each. A machete in a leather sheath. A plastic wallet, containing credit cards and a set of car keys.

He shook the cards and keys out on to the bed, adding them to the pile of stuff. Rummaging in the bag, he found another wallet. This one contained false passports for him, Anton and Luka. Three plane tickets. And a small book.

Milos took out the book, tilted it in the streetlight's watery glow. He'd told Anton to make sure he had it on the plane back to Dubrovnik. Reading it was to be his reward for killing Hazbi Dunja. Leaving it in Anton's care had been an act of faith, an expression of almost divine trust that the mission would succeed.

In Zrmanjagrad in 1995, when Milos had gone back into the house after the slaughter of his family, he had taken two things. His father's revolver. And this book.

He ran his fingers over the title: *Kraljevic Marko*. Beneath the words was an illustration of a bearded warrior on a winged horse. The gold leaf lettering glinted in the pale light.

It was an epic poem about Prince Marko, legendary hero of Serbia. It was Milos's favourite story from childhood. Marko was a brave knight with a fierce temper but a sympathetic heart. With his enemies he was ruthless. To his people he showed nothing but kindness. He dined with ogres and beat back the invading Turks. He fought with mace and sword, and vanquished all who challenged him.

The legend said that when the gun was invented,

Prince Marko had chosen to die, rather than fight with such a dishonourable weapon.

Milos stared at the two rifles on the bed. They were a last resort, he told himself. In order to truly honour his family—and the spirit of Prince Marko—he would have to deliver the final blow with his own hands. Only when he had soaked himself in Dunja's blood, could he be free.

But if fate left him no choice, he would have no qualms about shooting the murderer between the eyes.

He stuffed the book inside his jacket, along with the wallet. He would kill Dunja. He would be on that plane. He would get his reward.

From downstairs there came a dull thud.

Milos froze. The police couldn't be here already. Anyway, that hadn't sounded like a door being smashed in.

Moving slowly, he grabbed two boxes of ammunition and stuffed them in his pockets. He opened another box and quickly loaded the rifle with the telescopic sight. Leaving the other rifle, the machete and the rest of the ammunition on the bed, he crept out on to the landing.

He paused at the head of the stairs. He took a silent breath, sniffed the air. Leaning round the banister, he aimed the rifle down the stairs into the hall. The hall was empty. The front door was still closed and bolted. Slowly he descended. Halfway down, one of the treads creaked. He stopped, held his breath. Nothing moved. There was a draught round his ankles. Where was it coming from?

'Anton?' His voice was hoarse, little more than a whisper. He called again, louder this time.

The door to the front room was wide open. When he'd left Anton, it had been ajar. Pulse racing, he went the rest of the way down the stairs. Still nothing moved.

He followed the rifle into the front room. As he

rounded the door he dropped to one knee, to dodge the bullet that might be waiting for him. Easier, too, to fire on whoever might be in there.

Anton lay on the sofa, his throat cut wide open. Blood soaked his entire torso, the sofa cushions. It had even sprayed up the wall behind him. He was still alive, just. Bubbles popped in the raw meat of his neck; his left hand twitched like a needle at the end of the record. A needle with nowhere left to go.

Apart from Anton, the room was empty. The woman, Jelenka Levnicki, had gone, leaving behind a straggle of rope, her discarded coat and a pair of shoes. Milos stumbled over to the couch. He was well acquainted with death—usually of his own making—but this was different. This was Anton.

He took his old friend's hand and held it until the twitching stopped.

Swallowing hard, he checked the body. It didn't take him long to discover Anton's gun was missing.

The room stank of death.

Milos rushed down the hall, into the kitchen. The chair was tipped over on the floor. The back door was open. It swung soundlessly on its hinges. That was where the draught was coming from.

Dunja was gone.

From the front drive he heard an engine rev. The Jaguar! Tyres roared on the gravel. Car headlights splashed through the rippled glass of the front door, strobed across the hall ceiling. They were reversing the Jaguar out of the drive.

Milos started to run for the front door. Instantly, he checked himself. He had only a split-second to make the right decision.

Open the bolts, unlatch the door, chase them into the

road. They'll be gone before you get there, and it'll be too late to give chase.

You've got the rifle. Shoot the tyres.

It's dark. If you miss, they're gone.

Don't rely on the gun.

He turned on his heels and ran back up the stairs.

By the time he got to the bedroom, the headlights had disappeared. He grabbed the car keys off the bed and dashed back down the stairs. *That fucking translator! All that time admiring her athletic body and ignoring the fact she's probably a karate black-belt.*

On his way out of the back door he slowed. There, on the kitchen floor, lay the woman's pendant. That weird concoction of leather and crystal, like something the bedraggled gypsy women sold to tourists in the squares of Zagreb. Perhaps Romany. He almost stopped to pick it up. There was something talismanic about it. Maybe it would even bring him luck, lead him to her...

Fate, fate, fate.

But there was no time.

Fingers fisted over the keys, he dashed round the back of the house to the carport. With one yank, he pulled the PVC cover off the Ford Focus left there by Anton ten days earlier. He thumbed the key fob; the doors unlocked with a soft click. He opened the driver's door, tossed the wallet and the rifle into the passenger foot well, and fumbled the keys into the ignition. The starter motor turned over, faltered, turned over again. Ten cold nights had taken their toll. At last the engine caught. Milos kicked the accelerator and the car lurched out from under the carport and on to the drive. He flicked on the headlights. They illuminated the house opposite. And an empty road.

Left or right?

It came down to this, then: a simple game of chance. It seemed the outcome of his mission would be determined by fate alone.

Spraying gravel, he flicked the wheel to the right and urged the Focus off the drive. The avenue ahead was long and straight. In the distance, tiny but clearly visible under a sodium streetlight, was the Jaguar. It made a left turn and vanished.

He set off in pursuit.

For several minutes, he drove hard and furious, desperate to catch them up, force them off the road. But as he gained on the Jaguar, he started easing off on the accelerator. He was still far enough back that they hadn't spotted him yet. And there was still plenty that could go wrong.

All this time he'd underestimated them. Especially that translator. She must have been doubling up as a bodyguard, after all. Now she had Anton's gun. They were two to his one. He had to be careful.

He checked the fuel gauge. Full, thankfully. Not that he was surprised: Anton had always been thorough. The Focus would be taxed and insured, entirely legal. As long as he remained inside it, he would attract no undue attention.

As long as he held back, Dunja and Levnicki would have no idea he was on their tail.

Time enough still, he thought as he stalked the Jaguar through the quiet city streets. He glanced down at the rifle in the foot well. *But perhaps, in the end, I will have to resort to the bullet after all.*

Dunja had led him quite a dance across this foreign land. Milos would remain patient, but not for much longer. Soon the moment would come. When it did, he wouldn't hesitate. Whether Prince Marko approved or not, Hazbi Dunja's last sight in this world would be straight down the barrel of a gun.

Cat and mouse, they crossed the city of Leeds, finally rejoining the A1. Milos fought hard to keep the Jaguar in his sights, yet not draw attention to himself. There was no sign they'd spotted him. Once on the motorway, they just drove at a steady 100kph, heading north, north, north.

Edinburgh! Milos thought. *That's where he's due to speak tomorrow. Does he really think I will let him carry on as normal, after all that has happened?*

The longer the pursuit went on, the more he suspected Edinburgh was indeed Dunja's destination. As they crossed the Tweed and entered Scotland, he was convinced.

Milos had been to the UK many times before. But this was the first time he'd come this far north. As border crossings went, it was uneventful. No barbed-wire fence, no electric gate, no checkpoint. The signpost reading 'Welcome to Scotland' was gone almost before he'd spotted it.

It was strange. Everyone knew the English and the Scots hated each other's guts. So how did they manage to live side by side without blowing each other's brains out? Was the monarchy really the glue that held it all together? Would his own country ever know such peace?

His hands jerked at the wheel, pulling the Ford Focus back from the central reservation. He was dangerously tired.

He flicked on the radio, thumbed through the channels in search of something loud. He continued past American gangster rap and something sickly from a musical show. He hesitated at a phone-in where a woman was talking about being unfaithful to her husband in a clothes-store changing room. Finally, he settled on a station that appeared to be celebrating punk rock. The music was raw and angry. It suited his mood perfectly.

He turned up the volume and clenched his hands on the wheel until they hurt. The road was quiet. The lights of Berwick dwindled behind him. The night took him north.

He wished Anton were here.

Heavy guitar chords crashed out of the radio. The Clash started telling Milos that London was calling. Strangely, the punk music was starting to soothe him. He let his mind wander, remembering how Jelenka Levnicki had looked trussed up on the floor, with her arms behind her and her breasts thrust proudly forward...

He thumped the steering wheel. Of course! When Anton had tied her up, she'd filled up her lungs, expanded her chest. Then, when the knots were tight, she'd exhaled. It was the oldest magician's trick in the book. By the time she'd let all her breath out, the ropes hadn't been tight on her at all.

After I left him, Anton must have fallen asleep. I knew he looked tired. She got the ropes off, then when she heard me go upstairs, she crept into the kitchen and found the knife. She freed Dunja and cut poor Anton's throat into the bargain. Ruthless bitch!

Ruthless, yes. Also experienced. To work so quickly, so silently...

Where did they find a female commando?

Now he had two scores to settle. His hatred of Dunja outshone everything, it was the sun about which he still orbited after all these years. But now there was a new star in the sky: Jelenka Levnicki, the woman with the Roma pendant. What a curious pair they made.

What a hypocrite he would be, to denounce ethnic minorities in public, yet employ a Romany to keep him safe.

But then he'd always been a sly old bastard.

Double the revenge then: first family, then Anton.

Taking one hand off the wheel, Milos eased the little book out of his jacket. Prince Marko stared up at him, his face burning gold in the glow of the passing streetlamps. He kissed the cover of the book, placed it gently on the seat beside him.

Ahead, the Jaguar's tail-lights hung in the night, red and constant, leading him deeper and deeper into the land of the Celts.

19

March 1st
23:59
Parliament Square

WHEN he reached Parliament Square, Henry Worthington interrupted his short walk home. The sky was clear at last. As he gazed into space, the moon peeked out from behind St Stephen's Tower.

He huddled into his greatcoat, breathed in the chilly air. Silver moonlight cascaded across the elaborate Westminster roofline. Traffic rumbled, sporadic and sleepy. Far across the city, a siren wailed.

Slowly, with massive certainty, Big Ben chimed midnight.

For whom the bell tolls...

Henry shivered. There was something indomitable about the damned thing. No matter how often he heard the bell, he could never shake off the sense that it knew things he didn't. It had certainly been around longer than he had, and would no doubt still be here long after he was gone. Here, in the dead of night, he could almost believe it wasn't a clock at the top of the tower at all, but some infernal machine for manufacturing time itself.

He pulled his collar together round his neck and walked on. It wasn't far to the flat he kept near Westminster Cathedral, but it was a cold night and, after the day he'd had, sleep was all he wanted. He certainly didn't have time to get maudlin by the light of the moon.

As he skirted the manicured gardens of Parliament Square, he breathed deeply, hoping the cold night air might clear his head. But still the anxiety went round and round.

To begin with there was the body count. The only saving grace was that Hazbi Dunja wasn't among them. According to Brian Burfield, Charlie Paddon and his partner were confident Dunja was still alive—the fools even thought he might still turn up at Holyrood in the morning.

Henry couldn't stretch his imagination quite that far. But the fact that Dunja's body hadn't been found had to be a good thing. Didn't it?

The deaths were bad, of course. Especially the unfortunate taxi driver, who looked to be the only innocent victim in all this. But worse than that was the embarrassment. Looking back, it seemed to Henry he'd spent the whole day apologising. To the various Cabinet offices—including that of the Foreign Secretary, who was hopping mad at being made to look a fool in front of a pack of photographers. To the various groups Dunja had been due to meet with this afternoon. To the Scottish First Minister, Andrew Molloy. It had worn him down.

On top of everything there'd been bloody Jack McClintock. Jack Russell was right. Henry's brother-in-law had been snapping at his heels all day. They'd last spoken just an hour earlier. Jack had gleefully told him that the Story of the Disappearing Croatian Foreign Minister would be gracing the front pages of all the early editions. *The Times* would be running an analysis on pages two and three exploring a possible connection between Dunja's disappearance and fatal shootings at a service station near Doncaster.

When he'd finally put down the phone on Jack, Henry had just sat in his office, appreciating the quiet. By then, even the cleaners had left. Whitehall never truly switched off, but late at night the volume was cranked right down.

He had spent a while thinking about ways he might turn this one round, lifelines he might throw himself. He kept coming up short.

He had ended up staring at the screen on his laptop. The screensaver had kicked in again, projecting the familiar slideshow of Madeira. The sunshine had never looked so enticing.

Is it resignation after all? All I need is enough spin to give me a graceful retreat. Years of loyal service and all that. Unfortunate end to a glittering career. A few years in the sun and I might even forget I never got the OBE.

After all, he'd been looking forward to retirement long enough. Shame it was such a bitter pill. Maybe he could take Nick Luard and Brian Burfield down with him. That would sweeten it.

The trouble was, in the back of his mind, there was a nagging thought.

When I don't have Whitehall any more, what will I do?

It was academic. However this Dunja business turned out—and Henry could only see it ending in disaster—the damage was done. A thousand questions would be asked and he wasn't sure he had the answers any more. It was all out of his hands. He was now wholly reliant on the actions of a Croatian diplomat (who'd spent the entire day proving he was utterly unpredictable), a rabid Serbian assassin and a couple of SOD officers blundering around the countryside in their little red BMW.

Time to call it a night. The walk home always did him good. By the time he reached his front door, he'd usually left most of his fears behind him.

Outside Westminster Cathedral he stopped again. He'd never understood people who thought the cathedral beautiful. Personally, he thought it was ugly as sin—a candy-striped monstrosity that didn't know if it was meant to be a church or a mosque.

But, for all its faults, he loved it to bits. There was something unshakeable about it. Like St Paul's, it represented the true spirit of London. The spirit of survival.

Would he, Henry Worthington, survive this crisis? He didn't know. But as he stood beneath the cathedral's great arched facade, he felt his fears diminish. Not disappear—they were too great for that. But they shrank until they no longer troubled him as much. Perhaps this really was the end. If so, so be it. He'd had a good innings, given them a good run for their money. All good things came to an end.

Que sera, sera.

Convinced he'd just overseen the last great disaster of his career, Henry Worthington put the key in the lock of his Westminster flat and retired for the night.

Perhaps for good.

20

March 2nd
05:00
Central Police Station, Leeds

A SHARP click woke Charlie from a shallow sleep. He raised his head, felt a twinge in his neck and wondered if he'd heard his own spine. He rolled over, surprised not to find himself in his own bed, but on what felt like a park bench. Where the hell was he?

'Is the prisoner ready for his breakfast?'

The voice came from the other side of the room. Charlie blinked into the light (he never slept with the light on—why was it light?), looked round and finally remembered where he was.

He was in a police cell. The voice had come through the door slot. He'd been sleeping on the thinly padded bunk at the back of the cell. Rubbing his hand against the nape of his neck, he staggered to the door and bent to peer through the slot.

Bright eyes looked back at him from a ruddy face.

'I still say you could've found somewhere more comfortable,' said Charlie.

'Best room in the house, this one,' said DI Watts, through the slot. 'Want your breakfast before we take you out to the gallows?'

'Very funny. I'll take a strong tea if you've got one, though.'

'On its way. How's the uniform?'

Charlie looked down at the spare trousers he'd borrowed. They were a bit short in the leg but at least he wouldn't have to walk around with one knee torn open.

'It'll do,' he said. 'What's on the menu?'

At Watts's desk they shared hot tea and cold Pop-Tarts.

'I'd get us bacon butties,' Watts said, 'but the greasy spoon doesn't open for another hour. Still, you look like a man who likes a tart.'

Charlie pulled a face, but swallowed the sickly-sweet pastry all the same. And the tea got rid of the taste, mostly.

'There's something I've been meaning to ask you,' said Watts, wolfing his third Pop-Tart.

'Fire away.'

'What made you decide to join the Diplomatic Protection Group? Reason I ask is, well, I was thinking of joining myself.'

'First off,' said Charlie, 'we're not called the Diplomatic Protection Group any more.'

'Right, yeah, the…what was it, a merger? That when they started calling you a bunch of sods?'

Charlie nodded and smiled. There was no getting away from it. 'Got it in one.'

'So what was this merger all about? What changed?'

'In one respect, nothing much. Some of the lines of communication shifted, further up the chain at least. Budgets got switched around. A few of the bureaucrats got new job titles. They like that sort of thing. The idea was to streamline things, devolve responsibility back into the Met, even out to us grunts on the street. Brian Burfield—he's our Chief Super—thinks the security services just want us to do all their work for them, and maybe he's right. But I'm not complaining. It means I stay hands-on and that's just how I like it.'

Watts leaned back and burped. Charlie decided he liked DI Watts.

'So what's it like?' Watts said. 'Buzzing round the capital in those nobby red cars? Ever wish you could go and catch criminals instead of babysitting heads of state?'

Charlie laughed. 'Occasionally. Mostly we're too busy to think about things like that.' He hesitated. Watts was good material, he thought. A bluff Yorkshireman was just what the department needed. He might even mention his name to Brian.

'I thought maybe it was like being a museum guard,' said Watts. 'You know, like at the Royal Armouries, or one of those fancy art galleries. Making sure nobody nicks the paintings.'

Charlie laughed. 'That's not bad. Not bad at all. Only, what you've got to remember is this: it's not just any old picture SOD's guarding. It's the big one.' That made Watts stop and think. 'If you're interested, you should apply. Now, anything happen while I was asleep?'

'Not much. Forensics have finished up, coroner's been. Body's in the morgue. There'll be cameras outside the house before long. Good job it happened in the middle of the night. Helps us do our job before the press get a sniff.'

'I know what you mean.'

'We tracked down the owner of the house.' Watts leafed through some papers on his desk. 'Uh, one Ralph

Hanson. Bit of a local tycoon, quite well-known. Owns a chain of travel agencies, plus half the student properties you drove past last night. He's clean as far as we know. Rented the house through an agent called Levinson.'

'Have you spoken to Levinson?'

Watts delivered a malicious grin. 'Got him out of bed personally. Poor old boy's never opened his office so early. Turns out he's been renting the house in Belle Isle to the same man for the past three years. Surname of Chekhov. Never been any trouble, always pays his rent on time. When I described our friend with the open neckline, Levinson said, "That sounds like him."'

Charlie read through the report. Then he picked up the folder of photographs from the murder scene. 'Have you got these scanned in?' he said.

'Everything's digital,' said Watts. 'We have computers up north, you know.'

'Is there a PC I can use? I need to send some emails.'

Watts set him up at a spare desk. While he went to get more tea, Charlie collated the information the Leeds police had gathered on 'Chekhov' and composed an email to Brian.

See if this guy hooks up to Javor Milos anywhere down the line. I'm betting he used an alias but he's bound to have left a trail. The photos might help you get an ID. I don't think his neck always looked like it does in the pictures.

He attached two of the clearest scene-of-crime shots and sent the email to Brian Burfield at Scotland Yard. As a matter of course, Brian would copy it on to their first-base contact at MI5. Between them, they made a fine pair of bloodhounds.

This done, he sat back and watched the dawn threaten the sky beyond the yellowed vertical blinds. He picked up a pen and waggled it through his fingers, imagining he was Clint Eastwood with a silver dollar. He was still doing it when Watts came back with the tea.

'My sister can do that,' said Watts. 'Have you cracked the case yet?'

'If only,' he replied, putting down the pen. 'I was thinking: it seems pretty obvious this "Chekhov" character— if that's his real name—was part of Milos's operation. He was certainly the driver, and probably the fixer too. He kept the safe house ready, probably helped plan the operations. Everything from booking flights to moving guns. You can bet this isn't the first time these assassins have been through your fair city. The weapons cache in the bedroom is proof of that.'

'I know. Makes your toes curl.'

'It does that. What it doesn't do is get me any closer to working this one out. I've still got three people on the loose and no idea whether it's the good guys or the bad guys in charge.'

When he'd drunk his tea and refused another Pop-Tart, Charlie went out into the car park. Last night should have been gym night and he missed his regular workout—he needed to stretch his legs.

Eastwards the sky was growing pale. The early air was icy, but he welcomed it. He laced his fingers and worked his arms through a few isometric exercises, forcing the muscles to work against each other, encouraging his circulation to wake up.

To stop himself freezing, he jogged round the perimeter of the car park, enjoying the solitude. Beyond the fence, the city was quiet. Soon it would wake. Eventually, news would come in that Dunja had been spotted and the chase would continue. But for now it was just Charlie and the slowly brightening sky.

On his third circuit, his mobile rang.

So much for perfect peace, he thought.

The display read *ALEX*.

'Didn't wake you, did I?' she said. Her voice was low and quiet. She sounded very close.

'Where are you?'

'Security car park at Holyrood. I just arrived. Thought I'd give you a call before I check out the debating chamber.'

'You haven't been driving all night?'

She laughed. 'No, silly! I pulled over just north of Berwick, grabbed a couple of hours' kip. When I woke up I treated myself to coffee and chocolate from a twenty-four-hour petrol station. Have you had breakfast yet?'

'Yes. I don't want to talk about it.' Although, just for a second, he wished he could keep the conversation on such mundane matters as sleeping in cars and sickly-sweet breakfasts. Anything but dead bodies and missing diplomats.

Instead, he started filling her in on what he'd learned about the dead man they'd found in the house. 'I've no doubt he was Milos's fixer, so we've got one jigsaw piece that fits,' he said. 'But that doesn't help with all the others. The ones that are still rattling round the box.'

On the other end of the phone, Alex yawned. Charlie imagined her stretching in the front seat of the Zafira.

'All right,' she said. 'Let's go over it. One step at a time. What did we find at the house?'

Charlie sighed. 'You know what we found. You were there, remember?'

'Never mind that. Do as your Auntie Alex says, Charlie Paddon. Work it through. Give me the evidence.'

'Yes, miss.' She knew him too well. 'Right, okay. The SOC list runs something like this: in the front room we've got the body, obviously. Then there's the rope—tangled but not cut through—the coat, the pair of woman's shoes. The murder weapon, of course. Uh, forensics found long, dark hairs on the carpet, plus some fibres they're check-ing over. The hair probably belonged to the translator, Levnicki. In the kitchen we've got the toolkit, the chair and rope—cut through this time, probably with the same knife that was used to cut the fixer's throat. The mobile phone, smashed to pieces. Upstairs, a wardrobe had been moved to reveal a cache under the floorboards. Looks like it was cleared in a hurry—there was a Heckler & Koch left lying on the bed, plus ammo and a machete, an empty bag, plastic wallet…'

'Aren't you forgetting something?'

'What?'

'The pendant.'

'Oh, yes, right. It's funny—nobody seems to know quite what it is. One of the girls here thinks it's African but Watts says the shiny bits remind him of rosary beads. Oh, and when they turned it over they found a word stitched into the leather on the back: *táchiben*.

'What does that mean? Is it Croatian?'

'We're working in it. Look, Alex, I appreciate the ef-fort but I'm not sure this is getting us anywhere. What are your movements now?'

There was a pause, then a long sigh. 'I'm on my way into the main Scottish Parliament building. I radioed ahead, so security are expecting me. I'll run them through the checklist, make sure everything's set for Dunja's arrival. Tell everyone to work on the assumption it's business as usual.'

'Where there's life, there's hope.'

'And how do we know there *is* life, Charlie?'

That brought him up short. 'We don't. But as of this moment, Whitehall still hasn't cancelled the Dunja's speech. Until Henry Worthington officially tells us otherwise, the show goes on. So do your thing—get the place secure. If Dunja does appear, he could be in no safer hands.'

'Thanks, Charlie.'

Across the car park, a door swung open. Filling it—as he filled every doorway he stood in—was DI Watts.

'Chief Inspector Paddon,' he said. 'Scotland Yard on the line. Important.'

Trotting back to the station building, Charlie said to Alex, 'I've got to go. Sounds like Brian's on the phone.'

'Keep me posted.'

'Will do.'

DI Watts led him back to the desk he'd borrowed and had the call put through. Brian sounded even more tired than Charlie had felt when he'd crashed in the station cell.

'All right for you—some of us have been up all night,' he grumbled, when Charlie said yes, he had managed to get some sleep.

'What have you got, Brian?'

'You're not the only one struggling to put this thing together. While you've been snoring I've been thinking about mobiles.'

'Mobiles? Why?'

'It was you got me started, reporting the phone Milos smashed. The one you saw in the kitchen of that house? I got to thinking: why didn't we hear from Dunja all the time he was in that minicab? Damn taxi's got a radio, hasn't it?'

'The dispatcher told me the radio wasn't working. Nor was the satellite tracker. They were either switched off or malfunctioning.'

'Either way, it's odd. Anyway, I thought: what if it wasn't just Milos who had a phone? What if Dunja was carrying one as well?'

'If he did, wouldn't he have used it to call us?'

'You'd have thought so. Unless he had a reason for disappearing in the first place. I'm beginning to think our Croatian guest might have a hidden agenda.'

Charlie thought about this. It was some way short of an explanation, but Dunja's failure to contact the authorities was certainly odd. 'Go on,' he said.

'I got the techies working overtime, auditing all the mobile masts along the route taken by the minicab. What turned up was the number of the smashed phone—Milos's phone. No surprise there, since we know Milos was on the cab's tail all the way. But those hits also gave us a pattern we could use to search for any other phones being used along the same route. Eventually we found one. *Another* mobile phone, also unregistered, also used at intervals between Stansted and Leeds. Interestingly, several calls were made south of Doncaster, just before the incident at the service station. Another call was made in Leeds, shortly after you found the safe house.'

Charlie gripped the phone tight and stared at Watts across the desk. He'd known when Alex had mentioned it that mobiles might give them the break they needed.

'Anything else?' he said.

'You bet,' said Brian. 'Whoever's got that other

phone—and I'm assuming it's our missing Croatian—has just used it to make another call.'

'Where is he?'

'About forty miles south of Edinburgh.'

21

March 2nd
06:09
Cabinet Office, Whitehall

HENRY Worthington found early mornings harder to deal
with than late nights. Unfortunately, they came with the
territory. If he wasn't accommodating foreign time zones
he was facilitating another punishing itinerary. It didn't
leave much time for coffee and croissants.

It wasn't that Henry particularly liked his bed. He just
really liked his breakfast.

His night had been more or less sleepless. He'd told
the Morlocks on the night shift to call him if there were
any developments in the Dunja crisis. They had called
him once an hour. Sometimes twice. Seven phone calls
between the hours of one and five, none of them a scrap
of use. But you couldn't afford to ignore a single one, just
in case.

The most memorable had come in at three-fifteen.
One of the secretaries, Paddy Kaminski, had phoned to
tell him he hadn't heard anything from Leeds.

'Let me get this straight,' Henry had said, bleary-eyed

and fighting to control his temper. 'You've called to tell
me nothing's happened since you last called?'

'That's right, sir!'

The worst of it was, the half-wit had actually sounded
pleased with himself.

Henry had placed the phone gently in its cradle, then
let his head flop back into his duck-down pillows.

At five o'clock he'd cut his losses. After a quick
shower, he'd started the march back to Whitehall. He
went the long way, cutting through St James's Park so he
could visit the tiny pastry shop off Piccadilly—the one
that opened insanely early to cater for people like Henry,
who didn't know the meaning of normal office hours.

'The usual, Mister Henry?' said Dino, the astonish-
ingly fat octogenarian who ran the place.

'You know me too well, Dino.'

As Dino wrestled his bulk through the narrow space
behind the counter, Big Ben chimed the half hour. Steam
erupted as he worked the coffee machine. Henry closed
his eyes and inhaled. It was like a caffeine sauna.

'Can I please you with a pastry this morning, Mister
Henry?' Dino handed over a capped polystyrene cup.

'Too sweet for me, Dino. You know that.'

'Big sugar boost. Just what you need to get you going.'

'Ah, but you know what happens if you have too much
sugar all in one go.'

'What's that, Mister Henry?'

'You're just setting yourself up for one almighty crash.'

Henry left the pastry shop carrying his hot latte and
two warm croissants. If he kept up his usual brisk pace
they'd hold their temperature until he reached Whitehall.
It didn't seem right for a man to rush when he was walking to his own execution. But he hated cold coffee.

When he arrived Eileen's desk was empty. The brightly-buffed corridors were largely empty too.

Greeting him in his office were the morning papers.

He deposited his breakfast on his desk and spread the newspapers across the meeting table. It was exactly what he'd expected. But that didn't stop him getting mad.

'Croatian diplomat on the run', said the *Guardian*. The *Mail* led with a head-and-shoulders shot of Dunja under the headline, 'Have you seen this man?' The Sun went for the throat with, 'Cops Lose Croatian Bigwig'.

The papers that weren't running the story on the front page had it on page two. Some suggested Dunja's disappearance was down to the incompetence of what they loosely called the 'security services'. Some—including *The Times*—had even made a connection between Dunja's disappearance and the fatal shooting at the service station.

One thing was certain: the story had broken.

The Times' lead article was written, of course, by Jack McClintock. The headline was an uncharacteristically bold, 'The Runaway Minister'. Disguised as responsible journalism, the article was in fact another of Jack's blistering attacks on Whitehall. Without naming his sources (to Henry's relief), Jack claimed Dunja was missing because of an 'astonishing catalogue of blunders by British intelligence and SOD, formerly the Diplomatic Protection Group'. If Dunja was still alive it would be, he said, 'nothing short of a miracle'.

'All very breathless, Jack,' Henry muttered. 'For an encore you can tell us about the wailing and gnashing of teeth we'll get when the four horsemen of the Apocalypse turn up.'

He went back to his desk and flipped on the radio. To

his amazement, Jack McClintock's voice came out of the speaker. He nearly picked the radio up and threw it across the room.

Jack was being interviewed on Radio Four's *Today* programme. As Henry listened, the smug bastard trotted out an abridged version of his newspaper article. When the interviewer, Peter Pargeter, challenged him on the facts, he had the cheek to say he'd got the information 'on good authority from Whitehall sources at the highest level'.

Henry growled. He was pretty sure nobody knew about Jack having his direct line number. But everyone knew they were brothers-in-law. He played up his dislike of Jack, but suspected everyone thought he was doing just that: playing it up. 'It's true,' he sometimes wanted to shout, 'I really do wish my sister had never married the prat!'

The trouble was, Jack had his uses. And he'd never actually compromised the department, even when Henry had used him deliberately to leak information.

Plus, prat or not, Mary really did love him.

Feeling his blood pressure rise, Henry checked the time. He'd told the press office to send out the official press release at six-thirty. Let the *Today* team chew on *that* one. Twenty minutes to go. He supposed he ought to check in with SOD in the meantime, just in case there'd been a last-minute development, something Paddy Kaminski hadn't thought to mention.

Still fuming, he dialled Brian Burfield's direct line. As the phone rang, he kept half an ear on the radio. Peter Pargeter had abandoned Jack McClintock, but not the story. Now he was interviewing a Yorkshire woman who said she'd been at the service station where the shots were fired.

'Can you tell me what you saw?' said Pargeter.

'It were like something out the movies,' said the woman. 'All these guns. Then the motorbike blew up. Tell the truth, I didn't see much at all. I was hiding behind my car. I just heard all this banging. I kept my head down.'

'Did you see the police discharge their weapons?'

'Like I said, I didn't see much. I saw this policewoman afterwards. She was okay. I told her I felt all post-traumatic. They still made me pay for the petrol though.'

Henry snapped the radio off.

'Burfield,' said a voice at the other end of the phone.

'I thought being an island nation meant we could keep track of people coming into our country,' said Henry. 'Not to mention find them quickly when they got lost.'

'Henry,' Burfield said, 'before you start…'

'Before I start? I started yesterday, Brian. When was it, now? Oh yes: round about the time you lost my diplomat.'

'Henry, I…'

'Well, know this, Brian: I spent most of yesterday evening composing one of the hardest press releases I've ever had to write. It couldn't have been more painful if I'd written it in my own blood. It's due to go out in fifteen minutes and as far as I'm concerned it might as well have both our resignations attached to the bottom. Not only will it formally announce that Hazbi Dunja won't be addressing the Scottish Parliament—not to mention the banquet of haggis and neeps or whatever excruciating Celtic cuisine the Jocks have no doubt laid on for him—but it will also admit to serious security lapses, beginning with the failure to pick Dunja up in the first place and ending with the inability of our police force to find out where the hell he got to while they were looking the other way. Oh, plus the small matter of three people lying dead at a godforsaken service station somewhere up north. As shit goes, Brian, it's particularly brown and particularly deep and lets out an unbelievable stink, and you and I both know what piece of ventilation equipment it's about to come into contact with. We know that all you have to do now is tell me that Hazbi Dunja has been found dead— probably hanging by his neck from the Angel of the North with a Serbian bullet in his brain. Then we might as well all run for the hills.'

He broke off, flipped the top off his latte and took a sip. The coffee was barely lukewarm. It was the last straw. He would have slammed his tepid coffee down on the desk, but he didn't want to spoil the walnut veneer.

Cautiously, Brian Burfield said, 'I know it's been tough going, Henry, but…'

'But what, Brian?' He suddenly felt very, very tired.

'I've just come off the phone with Charlie Paddon. We've come up with something.'

'What sort of something?' Slowly, Henry released his grip on the cup. Burfield actually sounded positive—well, as positive as a born-pessimist ever did. As quickly as it had descended, the weight of exhaustion was lifting again.

Somewhere inside, he dared to hope.

'First off, don't send that press release. Cancel it, retract it, do whatever you have to do. Second, if you want to run anywhere, run to the airport. You were due in Scotland this morning, right?'

'Eileen booked the tickets.' Henry's mouth felt a little numb.

'Then use them. Get yourself up there, Henry. I've got a feeling our show might be back on the road.'

As Brian explained, Henry shot a glance at the carriage clock. His mind was racing.

Taxi to Stansted. At this time of day that's only forty-five minutes. I can still make the plane. Flight's less than an hour...

He realised Brian had asked him a question. 'I'm sorry, Brian,' he said. 'What was that?'

'I just said, "So, are you coming?"'

Henry didn't hesitate. 'Yes,' he said, and hung up.

As soon as he'd instructed his press office—on pain of death—to ditch the press release, he booked himself a taxi to Stansted. Normally, he'd have asked one of the secretaries to do it. But this new optimism felt fragile. He wanted to keep control of it. He scribbled a series of notes for Eileen, left voicemails on half a dozen phones, sent five emails copied to six different departments, then grabbed his coat off the stand and swept out.

In the doorway, he hesitated. Turning, he went back to his desk and picked up the paper bag containing the two croissants. They were as cold as the coffee, but he didn't care.

Grabbing *The Times* off the table, he folded it in two and hurled it across the room towards the wire wastebasket. It dropped a foot short.

Paddy Kaminski appeared at the door just in time to see the newspaper disappear.

'But I haven't photocopied the articles yet, sir,' he said.

'I think you'll find,' said Henry, 'that *The Times* prints more than one copy a day. Now, get out of my way—I've got a plane to catch.'

22

March 2nd
06:47
Leeds General Hospital

GOOD *to be back on the trail.*

Tracking Dunja's phone via the mobile masts had been the breakthrough they'd needed. Back at Scotland Yard, Brian Burfield had got busy with the map pins. Then, with the runaway diplomat's probable course established, he'd made some calls. First, he'd wangled the helicopter flight to Edinburgh for Charlie. Next, he'd convinced the Chief Constable of the Lothian and Borders police to put out an all-points alert on the Jaguar.

Fifteen minutes after speaking to Brian, Charlie was on the road again. He must have bashed his knee harder than he'd realised. It was aching like a bastard. At least it was only ten minutes to the helipad. The bad news was he'd have to leave the car in Leeds. The police helicopter was based at an RAF airfield some miles out of the city. As soon as Brian's request had come through, it had been scrambled. The quickest way to get Charlie into it was for them to rendezvous at the hospital helipad.

It was still early enough for Leeds to be largely free of traffic. He made good time. As he turned into the hospital grounds, he felt nothing but relief. Not only had they picked up Dunja's scent again, but he was heading for a rendezvous with Alex. If this crisis really was set to play itself out in Edinburgh, the team should be together.

As he slewed the BMW to a halt in the corner of the pad, a blue and yellow helicopter dropped from the sky, with the words POLICE and AMBULANCE emblazoned across the door. He grabbed the dossier he'd just printed off the BMW's printer and ran, head down, across the concrete. His knee protested, but he told himself to get a grip.

As Charlie strapped himself in, the pilot handed him a headset. 'Welcome aboard, sir,' he said, his voice tinny through the earpieces. 'Hear me all right?' Charlie gave him a thumbs-up. 'Then it's wagons roll!'

The helicopter juddered off the pad, and swung north. Less than a minute had passed since he'd parked the car. It was hard not to imagine himself in a Vietnam dust-off.

Despite the cabin soundproofing, the rotors thudded like machine-guns, vibrating in time with his pulse. Charlie peered out of the window. The BMW was a red splash on the rapidly-shrinking pad.

The pilot glanced back over his shoulder. 'Look like toys from above, don't they, sir?'

'They do,' Charlie replied.

'Spot yours a mile off, what with that fancy paint-job.'

'That's the idea.'

'Name's Bardot, by the way.'

'As in Brigitte?'

'Yup! First name's Douglas, but everybody calls me Doug.'

'I'm Charlie.' He thought for a minute. 'Your name's Douglas Bardot?'

'Yes, sir.'

'You don't have a tin leg, do you?'

'Ho ho, sir. Haven't heard that one before.'

Doug sliced the chopper up through low cloud and out into sunshine.

'If you want to get some kip, sir,' said Doug as they cleared the clouds, 'don't mind me.'

'Do I look that bad?' asked Charlie. He rubbed his chin and realised he hadn't shaved.

'Like shit, if you'll pardon me, sir.'

'Thanks. How long to Edinburgh?'

'Don't you worry, sir. This here's a McDonnell Douglas MD902 Explorer. She's got the latest gyro-stabilised cameras, thermal imaging, night-sun…the lot. On a good day she'll give you 250 klicks. Course, there's a headwind today so she'll be dragging her heels a bit.'

'In English, please?' Charlie said.

'Just over the hour, sir. I keep trying to do it in less. Never quite manage it though.'

'Tell you what,' said Charlie. 'Try a bit harder. Just for me.'

He turned his attention to the documents he'd brought from the car. It was information he'd asked Brian to fax over just before he left Leeds Central. The noise from the engine made it hard to concentrate. And Doug was right about the tiredness: he couldn't stop yawning. It was as if his body, with no choice but to sit still for the next hour, had decided to catch up on the sleep it had missed in the cell. But he had a hunch there was stuff in here he needed to know. He had most of the pieces of the puzzle now, he was sure of it.

'If Dunja's using his phone,' he'd said to Brian earlier. 'Who's calling? Not Whitehall, not us, nobody at Holyrood.'

'I don't know,' Brian had replied. 'Look, Charlie. I don't care if he's calling 0800 Hot Croatian Babes. All I know is he's got clear of Milos, forgotten about us and decided to drive himself. Catch him up. And when you do, don't let him out of your sight.'

Just before ringing off, Charlie had asked Brian to send through anything he'd got on Dunja's background. Specifically on his wartime experiences.

'He used to drive a tank, didn't he?' he'd said.

'Leave it with me,' Brian said. 'I'll send what I can. Just get to that chopper.'

Charlie leafed through the dossier.

There were plenty of stories from the war about Hazbi Dunja. The interesting thing was, they were all told by Dunja himself. No significant third-party corroboration. Not unusual in itself, until you remembered what a high profile he had these days. Surely some old war buddy would have come out of the woodwork by now?

Charlie's eyes lingered on a piece about a military advance that happened late on in the Croatians' War for Independence. Operation Thunder was designed to deal with the hundreds of thousands of Serbs still occupying Croatian territory. 'Deal with' meant drive out.

The Serbs claimed they were being ejected from land their families had owned for generations. As far as the Croatians were concerned, they were merely taking back what was rightfully theirs. It all depended on your point of view.

What made Operation Thunder controversial was the ruthlessness with which it was enacted. The Serbs weren't just ejected; they were bulldozed. Entire towns emptied before the oncoming tanks; those who didn't flee were slaughtered in their own homes. Reports of atrocities grew daily, but what was one more atrocity in a war truly understood by nobody outside the borders of Croatia—and precious few within?

Charlie traced his finger over a map showing the route taken by the Thunder tanks. Hazbi Dunja had been in charge of one of those tanks. What had he seen in those dark days? What had he done?

Maybe it isn't so strange old comrades haven't come forward to share their war stories. Maybe the stories were buried for a reason.

Speculation. None of it helped.

One thing's for sure: Hazbi Dunja's a man of action. Given everything that's happened since he arrived in the UK, we shouldn't be surprised he's decided to take his security into his own hands.

He checked his watch, looked out into the dawn. The chopper was noisy but the scenery was spectacular. Sutton Bank cast an immense westward shadow; beyond it, the North Yorkshire Moors crouched beneath late frost. The moors seemed to roll on forever, diminishing into the haze but never quite disappearing altogether. Charlie imagined he could see the North Sea, far in the distance.

That was the only trouble with London: no ocean. Having grown up on the Dorset coast, he needed a regular fix of wind and waves. Kathy had always said he didn't have blood in his veins, just brine. As for her—she hated the water.

Maybe that was why it hadn't worked out.

The pilot's voice interrupted his reverie.

'Got a young lady on the blower, sir.'

Charlie's first thought—insanely—was, *How does Kathy know where I am?*

'Who is it?' he said.

'Uh, a Sergeant Chappell, sir. She seems quite excited. Hold on a minute...here we go, putting you through.'

There was a pause, then an explosion of static. Charlie yanked the headset clear of his ears. When the static softened, he eased it back into place. 'Alex?' he said. 'Are you there?'

'...hear me, Charlie?'

'I hear you,' Charlie shouted into his mike. 'You're breaking up though.'

'...they could patch me through...technology for you...'

'Roger that. We'd do better with two cans and a piece of string. What's on your mind, partner?'

There was another flurry of static, then Alex's voice again, clearer now. '...clearing the ground ready for Dunja to arrive. They lost the Jag on its way into the city. Would you believe it's foggy up here?'

'Nothing would surprise me.'

'Anyway, we're assuming he's making his way to Holyrood. I've given up trying to second guess what he's up to. All I care about is making sure this place is secure for when he arrives.'

'And is it?'

'Pretty much. Holyrood's security is always switched on, as we know. Jim Connelly's running the show—you remember Jim from the US visit last year?'

'Yeah—he's a good man.'

'He's just back from holiday so he's pretty chilled out. Hell of a suntan. Anyway, I've just come out of the briefing so everyone's up to speed. We're doing a floor-walk in a minute but I needed to speak to you. I think I…' The static closed in again as the helicopter skimmed a bank of low cloud. Charlie waited in frustration. '…I mean?'

'Say again,' he said. 'I lost you for a minute there.'

'…I said, I've been on the phone to one of the curators at the National Galleries of Scotland. About that pendant. He wasn't too happy about the early-morning call.'

Charlie snorted. 'I bet he wasn't.'

'I got our friend in Leeds—DI Watts—to email the SOC photo of the pendant up to him. That was when he got interested.'

'It's just a pendant, Alex.'

More static, then, '…just it, it isn't. This curator chap got quite excited about it.'

'Is it African like we thought?'

'No. It's Romany.'

'*Romany?*'

'Yes. It was bugging me all the way up here, Charlie. The pendant didn't look like anything I'd seen before. The curator agreed: it's just a weird handmade thing— beautiful, but weird. But he said the first thing he thought when he saw it was "gypsy". Then he saw the word stitched on the back—*táchiben*—and that clinched it.'

'What does it mean?'

'It's the Roma word for "truth".'

'Language expert too, is he?'

'As it happens, yes. Lucky or what?'

She sounded so animated, Charlie didn't want to bring her down. But he couldn't see where this was going.

'Shouldn't you be starting your floor-walk?'

'Sod that, Charlie. Think about it. Don't you think it's odd? It's obvious the pendant belonged to Jelenka Levnicki. Who else? But it means she's a *Roma*,

Charlie. The Roma hate the Croatian authorities, what with the way they treat ethnic minorities and everything. What's a Roma doing working as a translator for the foreign minister? I thought they screened out people like her.'

'Maybe she isn't actually a Roma. Maybe she just likes the necklace.'

'It's not the kind of thing you "just like". I'm a girl, Charlie, in case you hadn't noticed. I know. A piece of jewellery like that, handmade…it's not a fashion statement—it's a…a *passion* statement.'

'Very clever. Look, Alex, I just don't think…' He stopped. 'Hold on. What colour hair did she have?'

'What?'

'Levnicki. What colour hair?'

'Uh, the hairs they found in the house were dark brown…'

'…and the woman I saw on the CCTV at Stansted had dark hair.'

Feverishly, Charlie leafed through the papers on his lap. He'd seen something earlier…there it was! A profile of Jelenka Levnicki, newly appointed as translator to Hazbi Dunja's office. She was young, in her early twenties. Fresh out of college. According to intelligence, the UK visit was her first assignment…

Dunja had never met her until they boarded the plane together. He wouldn't have known what she looked like.

…born in Dubrovnik, solid middle-class parents, high academic achiever…and there was a photo.

Jelenka Levnicki was blonde.

'Alex?' he said softly into the mike. 'I think I just solved the equation.'

'What?'

'The woman. It isn't her. It isn't Levnicki. She's an imposter. Alex, it's not just a Serbian assassin who wants Dunja's blood—he's got a Roma woman after him too.'

23

March 2nd
07:07
Scottish Parliament, Edinburgh

ALEX stood on the balcony of the Parliament building and watched the helicopter land in the distant grounds of Holyrood Palace. The palace building looked regal, formal, a complete contrast to the flamboyant curves of the modern architecture surrounding it. Some people said the Scottish Parliament looked like the Sydney Opera House. To Alex, it looked like a heap of fallen leaves.

Jim Connelly had sent a car over the road to the palace, to collect Charlie. Feeling curiously as if she were waiting for a date, Alex gripped the balcony handrail and kept checking her watch.

To her right, Arthur's Seat dominated the skyline. She knew the great hill had once been a volcano—that Edinburgh sat on the remains of umpteen volcanoes, in fact. That was why there wasn't a flat road in the city.

A seagull rose above the hill. Its piercing cry cut through the still morning mist. The fog that had dogged their every move had followed them to Holyrood, and showed little sign of shifting.

The Dunja crisis was coming to a head. She could feel it. Something was getting ready to blow.

The helicopter had vanished behind the trees. Charlie was on his way. As she made her way down to the security suite, her mobile bleeped. It was a text message from Lawrie.

HUBY HEER. ETNG BRKFST. WOT U DNG?

She smiled. Lawrie had mastered texting not because he thought the shorthand was cool, but because he was rubbish with keypads. Given his clumsy thumbs, it was a wonder his messages made any sense at all. She replied:

WORKING. BIG DAY. TELL U LATER. AX

Lawrie, clearly bored, wasn't letting it go at that.

FOGY IN ABRDN. WHR R U?

Alex was halfway down the stairwell. She stopped long enough to tell him:

EDINBURGH.

STONS THRW. C U 4 DNNR?

BOOK A TABLE. GOT TO GO.

Charlie was waiting for her in one of the small meeting rooms in the security suite. He looked up when she walked in, just as he had when she'd met him in the canteen in Leeds. Only now there was a thick shadow of stubble coating his jaw line. There were shadows beneath his eyes, which had lost their usual brightness.

'I'm waiting for Brian to call,' he said, indicating a phone on the table. 'He's been digging.' He sounded like he'd been gargling razor blades.

The phone rang. Charlie switched it to conference and Brian Burfield's voice crackled out of the speaker.

'Are you there, Charlie?'

'Here, boss. Alex, too.'

'Morning, sir,' said Alex.

'Good. Glad you're together. I need you both to hear this, all of it.'

'We're all ears,' said Charlie.

'All right. First off, well done, Charlie. You were right about the translator. The woman on the plane was an imposter. She assumed Jelenka Levnicki's identity, took advantage of the fact Levnicki was new to the department. Dunja had never met her. Nobody had. Everyone just assumed she was who she said she was.'

'What happened to the real Levnicki?' said Alex, sitting beside Charlie. They huddled close to the phone, and each other.

'I've just heard from the Croatian police. They went to her apartment, found the door had been forced, then patched shut again. When they broke in, they found Levnicki bound and gagged on the bathroom floor. She was in bad way: black eyes, broken nose…'

'Terrified out of her wits, I should think,' Alex put in.

'Hell of a first day in her new job, that's for certain. Anyway, we've had Interpol looking at CCTV pictures of our mystery woman. The ones we got from Stansted. Finally got a match this morning with a photofit they've had going round for a while. Looks like the woman's real name is Milka Rosic. A dyed-in-the-wool Roma and a political activist to boot. Used to be a gymnast, would you believe? She's been leading a guerrilla war against the Croatian authorities for the last eighteen months. Wanted for a number of terrorist attacks including letter bombs, at least two instances of kidnapping for both publicity and ransom…the list goes on.'

'She sounds like a dangerous woman.'

'Nobody likes her, not even her own side. The authorities want to arrest her and there's a sizeable Roma contingent that thinks she's doing their cause no favours at all. Of course, there's enough prepared to give her a hiding place when she demands it. You know what these people are like: they look after their own.'

'She must have some bottle,' Charlie said, 'to take the place of one of Dunja's people. I mean, it's not exactly keeping your head down, is it? It's a wonder the Croatians didn't spot her before she left the country.'

'What they call "hiding in plain sight",' said Brian. 'But you're right—she's a bold one.'

Alex looked at Charlie. 'How's the maths now?' she said.

He gave her a tired grin. 'I knew it was adding up while I was on the chopper. This just fills in the gaps.'

'What are you two saying?' said Brian, through the speaker.

'Nothing,' said Charlie. 'I was just thinking—the one thing we kept coming back to was why Dunja never called us up. All the way up the A1—all the way to Edinburgh for God's sake—not a peep. Now we know why: he was in this woman's palm from the second he walked off the plane.'

'But how did she manage it?' Alex said. 'On her own, I mean. Dunja's no fool. Plus he used to be a soldier, don't forget that. And—I can hardly believe I'm saying this— she's only a woman.'

Charlie shrugged. 'She's a guerrilla fighter. A terror-ist. The fact she's got this far proves she knows what she's doing. She probably smuggled a weapon on to the plane. Worked the diplomatic immunity rules to her advantage. It wouldn't be the first time. And as Dunja's translator she was never going to be the star of the show. All eyes were on Dunja himself—including ours. Nobody was inter-ested in the supporting act.'

'She must have pulled a gun as soon as they got in the minicab at Stansted,' Alex said. 'Still, she must be a hard case, to keep Dunja subdued all that time. The taxi driver, too.'

'The Croatian Foreign Office reports that Dunja's re-covering from a bout of the flu,' Brian said. 'That won't have helped.'

'And she probably had friends here…' Charlie sud-denly slapped his hand down on the table. 'Of course! The mystery rifleman in the Range Rover! *That's* why he was shooting at Milos. That's what the whole shoot-out was about: the two kidnap teams—Milos's and Rosic's— were slugging it out for the same prize. And we walked right into the middle of it.'

'I wonder if Milos knew about Rosic's true identity,' said Alex. She could almost hear Charlie's brain ticking over that one.

'I don't think so,' he said at last. 'Not at first, anyway. When the Jaguar drove away from the service station,

Milos was in charge. I think he only discovered who she really was when they reached the house in Leeds. When she cut his partner's throat.'

'So who's Dunja with now? Milos or Rosic?' said Alex.

Charlie stood, ran his hands through his hair. 'My gut says Rosic,' he said. 'It doesn't explain why she's bringing him to Edinburgh, but if Milos had him, he'd be dead already. The man's an assassin, pure and simple.'

'Not quite so simple,' Alex murmured. 'Remember the tool bag in the kitchen? It looked like a makeshift torture chamber to me. And Brian, wasn't there something on your initial briefing sheet about Milos having some kind of grudge against Dunja?'

'Yes,' Brian said. 'We never got to the bottom of it. We know that before he started shooting people, Milos wrote pamphlets for the Serbian underground. In a couple of them he hinted he'd encountered Dunja in the war. But he never elaborated. Bottom line is, he's a killer, just like Milka Rosic. Doesn't matter which one pulls the trigger—Hazbi Dunja's a dead man either way.'

By now Charlie was pacing up and down. Alex could see him working his brain as hard as he was his feet. But it wasn't getting him anywhere.

The security suite was at ground level. From down here, the green flank of Arthur's Seat looked bigger than ever. Alex could see walkers on it already. She imagined the locals all gathering to do tai-chi on the summit before breakfast. Afterwards, they could stroll down the shallow southern slope to Holyrood Park…

'It *is* Rosic who's got him,' she said quietly.

'Say again,' said Brian. Charlie stopped pacing, lowered his hands, stared at her.

'What've you got, Alex?' he said.

She gave him a grim smile. 'It's staring us in the face. We even covered it in this morning's security briefing. It's so obvious—I don't know why I didn't think of it before.'

'Ditch the suspense, Alex,' said Brian. 'We're running out of time.'

'Holyrood Park! Don't you remember, Brian? You told me yourself only yesterday. The local police were concerned it might be a security threat but decided to let it go. And so they're still here!'

'Who?' said Charlie, practically beside himself.

'The Romanies! They set up a travellers' camp in Holyrood Park. Rosie must have friends there. Not to mention something in mind. And whatever it is, she's about to do it. Right under our noses.'

24

March 2nd
08:17
Holyrood Park, Edinburgh

HE STUDIED the index finger of his right hand. The tip of
the finger had turned black. He'd seen frostbite plenty of
times, rotting the extremities of resistance fighters
brought back from the mountains above Zrmanjagrad.
They had suffered much worse than this. Soon he would
make their sacrifice worthwhile.

It was the same finger that Hazbi Dunja had suffered
his injury to. The irony was not lost on him. Javor Milos
rested the rifle on the rocky crag. He cupped his hands,
blew into them. His breath was hot and moist, and did
nothing to ease the pain. The gloveless ride up the A1 on
that Honda…crawling across the tarmac in the service
station…it had all taken its toll. Where they weren't
black, his fingers were purple. When he touched the skin
he felt nothing; when he flexed them it was agony. He
thrust them into his armpits, willing his blood to fill them
with heat. There was one more job he needed them for.

Slowly, his hands revived. He picked up the rifle and

settled back into the position he'd been holding for the last two hours.

Soon, he thought. *Very soon.*

The punk music had done a good job of keeping him awake on the long drive north. At some point in the night, it had segued into a session with a trio of Hungarian singers. The women sang strange, ululating harmonies, which reminded him of home. The music was powerful. It was like something from another realm. It made him feel strong again.

His sense of dislocation had grown when he'd reached the outskirts of Edinburgh. Instead of driving straight into the city centre, the Jaguar had meandered through patchy fog to a park. Beyond the park rose a grassy hill, huge in the intermittent moonlight.

On a patch of scrubland just inside the park was a sprawl of caravans. A travellers' camp. Milos parked the Focus beneath a line of trees and watched as the Jaguar pulled off the road and into the camp. Once more he was forced to revise his opinion of the translator. First the Romany pendant, now this… There was no doubt the woman was Roma, in which case she was as much Hazbi Dunja's enemy as he.

Perhaps Hazbi Dunja hadn't escaped captivity at all. Perhaps he'd just exchanged one prison guard for another.

He allowed himself a bitter grin. A feisty woman who hated the same people he did. And what a body! On a different day, in different circumstances…what a team they might have made.

He kept the motor running, reluctant to let the car lose its heat. The Jaguar had vanished. Most of the caravans were in darkness. There was nobody about. He rested his aching hand on the door latch.

If I find the car, I will find them. I have the rifle. Surprise will be on my side.

But in this darkness, how long would it take him to locate the Jaguar? The camp looked quiet, but he knew what these Roma scum were like. However peaceful the place looked, they would still have guards posted. Armed he might be, but he was just one man. And a tired man at that.

If she has brought him here, it is because she wants to make some kind of scene at the Scottish Parliament. Why else take such a risk?

It was just after midnight. If the woman was indeed hoping to disrupt the Parliament, she would surely wait for morning to make her move. In daylight, at least, he stood a chance.

He could afford to wait a little longer.

He circled the camp until he found a sheltered spot to pull off the road. A short track dipped between overhanging trees. Nobody would find him here. His mind began to wander, and carried him through a series of visions about warrior women on winged horses. They rode through the sky over vast mountains, chasing Milos through the clouds. The horses' wingbeats sounded like the thunder of tanks…

He woke with a start and checked the time. How long had he been asleep? What if his quarry had fled? It was four o'clock. Blackness still engulfed the Romany camp. Some inner certainty told him Dunja was still there, held captive in one of the caravans.

Time to move.

Rubbing his fingers—without the heat from the engine, the cold had gripped them again—he took the rifle and started walking up into the woods. As an afterthought, he returned to the car and picked up the book.

Even in the darkness, it didn't take him long to find the perfect spot. He was an assassin: vantage points were his speciality. A crag of rock jutted from a shallow rise, free of trees. The rock gave him both cover and a clear line of sight down to the lane leading into the camp. When Dunja left in the morning, it would have to be along that lane. And Milos would have a ringside seat.

The night made it hard to judge the distance. It was certainly no more than four hundred metres. That was fine. The Heckler & Koch had a telescopic sight and fired hefty 7.62mm shells. The last time he'd fired a weapon like this, he'd achieved millimetre accuracy at five hundred metres. As long as he could get Dunja in the crosshairs, he was a dead man.

Again he rubbed his fingers.

Assuming I can pull the trigger, that is.

He settled down to wait. Gradually, the pain went away. The cold numbed his body, but it didn't matter. All that mattered was that he was in the right place, waiting for the right time, with his weapon chocked against his shoulder. As the sky slowly began to grow light, he felt his spirit lift in response. In the back of his mind, the Hungarian women sang. It didn't even matter that he was resorting to the gun. He knew Prince Marko would understand.

Dawn crept between the trees. Caravan doors opened; smoke rose through the lingering mist. From beneath a rusting trailer burst three mongrel dogs, yapping and howling as they chased each other in a canine tornado. Their barking floated up to Milos on the morning air. Women in coloured shawls carried jugs, or bundles of washing. The men stood smoking in the half-light, sharing words beneath the striped awnings.

Soon there would be people on the hill, too. These

Scots were mad for their mountains. He'd heard there were some old men who climbed Ben Nevis every day, just for pleasure. For Milos, mountains were where the people were forced to flee, to hide, to die. The idea of them having any recreational value was insane.

This was no mountain, but it would attract walkers all the same, soft city folk keen to convince themselves they were hardy, outdoor types. Sooner or later, he'd be discovered.

But not yet.

A vehicle pulled out from behind a row of caravans. Milos hunched forward, eased his finger through the trigger guard. Through the telescopic sight, the car was enormous. He tracked it with the rifle, homing in on the driver.

The car was a rusty Nissan, driven by an old geezer with a Zapata moustache. It coughed its way up the lane and vanished round the corner behind the trees. Relaxing, Milos lowered the rifle. But he kept his eyes moving, scanning the camp, looking for that critical clue.

Waiting.

25

March 2nd
08:26
Holyrood Park, Edinburgh

IN A CROUCH, Charlie crept through the trees. Further up the hill, three Scottish firearms officers were completing their recce of the hillside. A hunch had sent him lower, directly towards the Romany camp. There was something about the lie of the land here, something that drew him down…

His fatigue had transformed into a kind of grim euphoria. He knew it was adrenaline, of course; he knew he'd pay later.

The camp was larger than he had expected. This was no handful of caravans, but more like a mobile town. Or a medieval joust, with its rows of awnings, its lines of washing strung like pennants.

He put his hand in his pocket, found the little silver amulet from the Royal Armouries. He'd never thought of it as a lucky charm, but he gave it a stroke all the same. It couldn't do any harm.

He studied the camp. It was surprising how similar the

caravans were—most white, a few silver and grey. Was Hazbi Dunja really down there? Was he tied up in one of the vans? Was Milka Rosic with him, composing some kind of ransom note to present to the Scottish Parliament?

Or did she intend to deliver his body to the Parliament's door?

Part of him wanted to take a squad of armed officers straight down into the camp, to start searching the cara-vans. But the situation was more complicated than that. While he was out here doing his preliminary sweep, a specialist team was being assembled back at Holyrood, on the other side of the hill. Given the track records of both Javor Milos and Milka Rosic—and given what had happened at the service station—there was no telling what kind of firepower the two parties might be holding in reserve.

Charlie had seen some of the headlines in the morn-ing papers. He could just imagine Henry Worthington tearing his hair out. But they were nothing compared to what might be on the news by tonight.

He paced downslope through the trees, following a narrow path. His knee felt like someone had filled it with ground glass—he'd have to get it looked at when all this was over. The thick vegetation seemed to thrum with eerie silence. He half-expected to send a brace of grouse whirring into the sky, or find himself confronted by a stag. But, glorious as it was, this was still a city park. All he saw were a couple of squirrels and a heap of discarded beer cans.

The slope steepened. He started to trot, ignoring the pain.

He met a path. To his left, it dropped steeply into a stand of young pine trees. It would lead, eventually, round behind the camp. To his right the terrain was more open, the path more even.

He went left.

The light was still dawn-poor; the air cold. Charlie's breath followed him in a thin ribbon. As he neared the trees he slowed still further. They would give him cover. They were also a perfect place for an attacker to conceal himself.

The path through the thicket was covered in dead bracken and fallen needles. It was soft and damp, and swallowed the sound of his footfalls. He stopped frequently to peer into the gloom. Every shadow was a potential hiding place, every turn a potential trap.

All he could see of the camp now was the occasional flash of colour through the branches. The path actually seemed to be taking him away from the travellers. Maybe he shouldn't have come this way after all.

Five more minutes, then I'll turn back.

The path rose sharply and the camp disappeared altogether. Then came an unexpected turn, a sudden descent and the edge of the woods.

The trees thinned out rapidly into open ground. The shallow slope afforded a perfect view of the camp. Charlie could see the smoke rising as breakfasts were cooked. His stomach rumbled. People were moving between the caravans. Charlie watched a battered Nissan jolt its way down the access lane. Shortly after it had left, he heard another motor start up.

A perfect view.

A big, black car glided round the back of the camp, visible only as it appeared fleetingly through the gaps between the caravans.

Fifty metres down the hill, a rocky crag broke clear of

the soil beneath an old Scots pine. It was a sheltered spot, thick with shadows. Charlie started limping towards it. His knee really was playing up now.

Suddenly, one of the shadows moved. Charlie's hand slipped inside his jacket.

26

March 2ⁿᵈ
08:28
Holyrood Park, Edinburgh

MILOS watched the black car turn between two of the cara-vans. Suspension bouncing, it rolled over the scrubby grass towards the lane. Once more he touched his aching finger to the trigger of the Heckler & Koch. Nestling the rifle's stock against his shoulder, he peered through the sight.

The car was a Mercedes, old, but well looked-after. Even through the mist its paintwork gleamed. At the wheel was a young man in a black suit and tie.

In the back was Hazbi Dunja.

The car was travelling slowly over the bumpy ground. It was easy to track it laterally with the rifle, impossible to anticipate the bumps and jolts as it dropped into the potholes. Dunja's head slipped through the crosshairs, up and down, never quite holding still. Milos thought about shooting for the tyres, or even a burst of fire at the driver, anything to stop the car. No. If he missed, Dunja would be able to slip through his grasp again. That wasn't going to happen.

The road was tarmac. When the car reached it, the shot would be easy.

Occasionally, Dunja's face vanished behind other objects: sheets hung out despite the fog, awnings, the heads of the Romanies going about their morning business. Milos was used to such visual clutter, and didn't let it upset his aim. The Mercedes would be in the clear soon enough. There would be nothing between him and his target but three millimetres of glass.

And that wouldn't stop a 7.62 mm bullet.

As the black car passed behind the final row of washing, something changed.

Milos froze. He'd heard nothing, seen nothing. All the same, he knew something was wrong. He felt it in his guts. He was an assassin, a hunter.

And, like all good hunters, he knew when he was being hunted.

Through the telescopic sight, he could see the Mercedes moving into the clear. It was still bouncing up and down. In three seconds it would be on the tarmac.

There is someone behind me.

He shifted his weight to the left, turned his knee inwards to support his body. The rifle didn't move a centimetre. His body was coiled, ready to spring.

In one second he would have a clear shot.

'Armed police! Drop your weapon!'

The spring uncoiled. Snakelike, Milos rose and spun. He moved swiftly, smoothly, despite the muscle cramps, the awful, bone-chilling cold, the agony in his hands.

As he rose from his crouch, his gaze locked on the eyes of a tall, broad-shouldered man standing less than ten metres away. The eyes were tired and a little bloodshot. Milos imagined his must look just the same. The policeman's legs were set a little apart, knees a little bent. He was leaning slightly, favouring his left leg. One hand gripped the butt of a handgun—a Glock. The other steadied the wrist. The muzzle of the gun was a tiny black eye, staring straight at Milos. It didn't shake.

He'd stared into those eyes before: the previous day, at the service station. When he'd been climbing into the Jaguar, he'd seen this man—this policeman—through the flames from the burning motorbike. The policeman must have trailed him all the way here.

Nice work, cop, he thought.

'Drop your weapon or I open fire,' the policeman shouted.

'Yes, okay,' Milos mumbled, holding out his left hand, fingers splayed.

'Do it now!' shouted the cop.

Milos shifted his weight and brought the rifle to bear. His swollen finger tightened on the trigger. But his muscles were more obedient than he'd given them credit: the rifle swung past its target, and a bullet rang out against a tree trunk behind his assailant.

The policeman's bullet hit his shoulder like a sledgehammer. His right arm flew out; the rifle was thrown from his grasp and went clattering over the rocks and away down the hill. He tried to hitch in a breath but his chest was in a vice. For a second, he thought his heart had stopped.

He managed to take a single step forward before he was hit again, this time by shoulder of the charging cop. Milos felt his wounded arm wrenched up behind his back and a leg hooked behind his knees. He fell sideways, felt what was left of his breath explode from his lungs. The policeman rolled him on to his front, pulled his other arm round. Cold metal handcuffs snapped around one of his wrists.

His face was pressed against something hard. The rock, he supposed. Then he saw it was the book. It had fallen from his pocket. On the cover, astride his winged horse, Prince Marko raised his sword. The sword was spotted with blood. Milos's blood.

Far down the hill, out of reach, lay the rifle. The dishonourable gun. He felt his other wrist being manoeuvred into position

'You have the right to remain silent…' the policeman started to say.

Milos arched his spine and kicked backwards. His boot hit something hard—the policeman's knee, he guessed. The cop cried out. The hand that had been holding his wrists let go.

Rolling on to his back, he lashed out again. The policeman dodged and Milos's foot whistled through thin air. The policeman's face was contorted with pain; his hand was groping at his left knee. Milos scrambled towards him, grabbed his boot with his hands, the cuffs dangling off one wrist, and twisted his leg. The policeman's other boot smashed into his jaw, knocking him back, head full of splintered sound.

The rifle!

He started crawling, over the rock then down into a damp puddle of leaves. The gun looked a million miles away. He could make it.

The cop was following him, breathing hard. Milos tried to stand, but felt his legs give way. He threw out his hands for support, but a sharp jag of rock came up out of the leaves and hammered into the ribs he'd bruised from falling off the motorbike—and which had taken a second beating when the cop had piled into him. The impact was pure agony. Milos felt the policeman seize the cuffs again, then his face was forced down into the ground. He tried to breathe and couldn't. The world went grey.

'Right,' the policeman panted. 'We'll try that again. Once more with feeling. You have the right…'

A thousand Serbian curses bubbled up inside his gut. Milos wanted to shout at the cop, call him a bastard, spit in his face. But his chest was on fire and all he could manage was a feeble, 'Fuck you…'

The policeman paused, then carried on with his caution: '…to remain silent. Anything you say…'

Milos closed his eyes and blanked out the words. They didn't matter. He was utterly spent. He had failed. It was over.

He was hauled to his feet. The cop was stronger than he looked. Casting a glance back towards the Romany camp, he saw that the black Mercedes had disappeared.

Hazbi Dunja had had slipped through Javor Milos's frostbitten fingers forever.

27

March 2nd
08:52
Scottish Parliament, Edinburgh

HE'D MADE the flight by the skin of his teeth. The check-in was closing when he got to Stansted, but he waved a bunch of official papers and greased his way through. On the plane his good fortune continued to hold: it turned out to be some kind of anniversary flight for the airline, so it was free champagne all round. He even got a window seat.

Halfway to Edinburgh—and halfway through the miniature airline breakfast—the pilot came over the loudspeaker to tell them the east coast was fog-bound. There was a chance they might have to divert to Glasgow.

Henry groaned. What an irony that would be!

He flagged down a passing stewardess.

'We're not really landing in Glasgow, are we?' he said.

'Well, between you and me, I think it's just the captain keeping his options open,' she said. 'It sounds like the fog's only patchy. Keep your fingers crossed and we might be in luck.'

He devoured the rest of his breakfast. The egg might have been laid by a pigeon and the black pudding could have doubled for a bath plug. He didn't care. It was all going to come out all right. He knew it was.

Approaching Edinburgh, Henry gazed down at the fog. From up here it looked pretty solid; he started to wonder if they'd be diverted after all. But it turned out to be thinner than it looked. As the plane made its final descent, the cloud seemed to break apart. When they landed, it was in the lightest of Scotch mists.

As the plane taxied in, his phone rang.

'Henry, it's Brian. Where are you?'

'I've just landed. Perhaps if you spent more time checking on your real charges, we might not be….'

'We've got Milos,' said Burfield.

Henry wasn't going to allow himself to hope. There was something in Burfield's tone that told him this wasn't the final word he wanted.

'And, dare I ask, what about Dunja?'

Burfield was silent for a moment. 'I think we're close. Paddon is on the ground now. We may not have him by nine, but we'll have him soon enough.'

'Let's just make sure this isn't a funeral, Brian,' he said. 'Keep me updated.'

Henry spotted a driver waiting at the arrivals gate. He was holding a wipe-board bearing the name HENRY WORTHINGTON.

Why couldn't things have gone this smoothly at Heathrow yesterday morning? thought Henry, as the driver opened the door to the limo. *Trust the Jocks to show us how things should be done.*

Beneath the glowering slopes of Arthur's Seat, the limo hit traffic.

McRush Hour, thought Henry. *Well, my luck couldn't hold forever.*

Then again, perhaps it could. At the far end of a gridlocked Canongate, a flashing blue light emerged. As Henry watched, it began to fight its way through the traffic towards his limo. He sat back in the leather upholstery, closed his eyes and waited for the cavalry.

The police car reached the limo and made a swift U-turn. Ahead, like a miracle, the traffic parted. The limo driver accelerated into the police car's wake and in less than a minute had delivered Henry to the main entrance of the Scottish Parliament.

For once in his life he actually felt like a VIP.

Waiting to greet him was Sergeant Alex Chappell. She looked irritatingly fresh, considering, and he fought back the urge to lambast the SOD operation. There would be time for that later.

'Glad you're here, sir,' she said, as he climbed out of the car. 'How was your flight?'

'Do you know,' said Henry, 'it was as smooth as anything.'

'That's good.' Alex seemed distracted. She was making the right noises but her attention was anywhere but on Henry. 'Touch wood, the pieces are falling into place here.'

Her bonhomie was getting on Henry's nerves.

'I'd say there is still a rather crucial piece missing, wouldn't you? I can't quite believe I've let Burfield talk me into coming all the way up here.'

Chappell flushed and looked ready to offer a comeback, when her attention was caught by something behind him.

There was a scrum of photographers at the side of the road. A few snapped at Henry as he lifted his coat and briefcase from the car; most ignored him. He didn't know whether to be offended, or grateful he wasn't a media star.

'I suppose we'd better go inside,' he said, slamming the door shut. 'You can bring me up to speed on any new developments since I spoke to Brian.'

'"Speed" is the word, sir,' Alex replied. 'Things have been moving so fast that…'

She stopped. Like a flock of starlings, the photographers had turned to face down the drive. Another car was approaching: a shiny black Mercedes. As soon as Henry's limo pulled away, the Mercedes took its place. The photographers crowded in. The rear passenger door of the Mercedes opened. A pair of legs emerged. They belonged to a tall man with long hair combed over a noticeable bald spot.

The Croatian Foreign Minister, Hazbi Dunja.

Henry felt his jaw hanging slack. He closed it with a snap and extended his hand.

'It's a great pleasure to see you safely arrived in Scotland, sir,' he said. 'May I take the opportunity to welcome you officially on behalf of the British government, the Scottish Parliament and, of course, Her Majesty the Queen.'

Dunja stared at him. For a moment, he seemed to stare through him. Then he shook Henry's hand and said, in faltering English, 'It is pleasure to be here. Thank you.'

Ignoring the shouts of the photographers and the flashes from their cameras, Henry started ushering Dunja towards the huge canopy shielding the entrance doors. Dunja walked stiffly, like a man with arthritis. His high forehead was beaded with sweat and his cheeks were flushed.

'Are you all right, Mr Dunja?' he said, as he tried to hurry the man along—without success.

'A small fever,' Dunja replied. 'I suffer with the influenza. All will be better when I make the speech.'

Henry felt someone tugging at his sleeve. It was Alex Chappell. He resisted the urge to brush her away.

'What is it?' he hissed.

'With respect, sir,' said Alex, 'what the hell are you doing?'

'I am escorting our VIP into the Scottish Parliament, Sergeant Chappell. Please allow me to...'

'But we can't just carry on as if nothing's happened! Have you seen the state of him? At the very least, we need to carry out a debrief. Then there's the...'

'Is there a problem?' said Dunja, stumbling to a halt. Behind them, the photographers were closing in. Behind the photographers, a phalanx of policemen was belatedly trying to form a cordon.

Henry was about to reply when Alex stepped forward. 'Sir, given everything that's happened, I'm still very concerned about your security. We need to get you inside, where we can look after you properly. The group who abducted you yesterday may still be at large. As long as we remain in the open, you are vulnerable.'

Dunja looked right at Alex. 'The speech must go ahead,' he said. 'Until I speak, nothing else is important.'

'Shouldn't we at least talk about what happened yesterday, sir? Forgive me, but there are a lot of unanswered questions.'

'This I am aware of, officer. I will talk with you after the speech. Then all will be clear. Until then, please, let me proceed.'

Henry looked from one to the other, feeling left out.

'Very well, sir,' said Alex. 'But I will ask you this one more time: are you sure you want to go ahead?'

'I have never been more certain about anything,' said Hazbi Dunja. 'Not in all my life.'

Alex's shoulders dropped. So did her right hand—towards her gun. 'Then let's get inside,' she said. 'After you, sir.'

'I'm sure we'll have plenty of time for explanations later,' Henry said smoothly as they moved under the shadow of the canopy. Alex shadowed Dunja closely, her eyes everywhere.

A knot of Scottish MPs was waiting at the doors. As Dunja was swallowed up, Alex remained doggedly beside him. *Give the man some space*, thought Henry. He decided not to go in just yet; instead he loitered under the canopy, letting the relief flood over him.

The police had finally got the press in check. Behind the uniforms, the cameras continued to flash. Every lens was pointed at Hazbi Dunja; nobody was interested in Henry Worthington any more. That was fine by Henry. But during his short encounter with Dunja he'd had his picture taken at least a dozen times. One or two shots might end up on a news editor's desk.

Nothing like column inches to save a career, he thought. *Jack McClintock, you'd better be on a starvation diet today. Because tomorrow you'll be eating the biggest portion of humble pie that was ever served.*

As for Brian Burfield—well, it looked like the grumpy little short-arse had been right to get him up here after all. Henry imagined Burfield pacing his office at Scotland Yard, as yet unaware his gamble had paid off.

He pulled his mobile out of his jacket pocket. Time to put the SOD Chief Superintendent out of his misery. After all the toadying phone calls he'd had to make yesterday, this one was going to make a pleasant change.

'Burfield?' he said when the Chief Superintendent picked up the phone. 'Good news: Lady Luck has been with us all morning. And it looks like she's here to stay.'

28

March 2nd
08:58
Holyrood Park, Edinburgh

CHARLIE'S hand was on his belt, ready to grab the Glock if he needed to. Three lads on bikes escorted him into the travellers' camp. They'd appeared from nowhere as he approached the first caravan, as if he'd snagged some invisible tripwire. They zigzagged in front of him, heads high, tyres spraying dirt. The oldest looked about ten, but there was a hint of menace about all of them. Still, they weren't his problem.

'Who's fastest out of you three, then?' Charlie said. None of them replied, but the youngest giggled and swerved in front of him, nearly taking off his toes.

As he limped between the caravans, he was surprised at how permanent the place felt. The vans were pulled up in loose rows, creating informal streets. Most sported long aluminium poles topped with TV aerials. In the alleys between the vans, sheets and woollens hung limp on washing lines; some of these extended right across the middle of the main 'street'. Behind most of the small

NICK CURTIS 211

windows were cheerful curtains and, on the sills, china knickknacks.

Faces peered through some of the curtains. Some of the people looked suspicious; most seemed simply curious. Charlie tried to guess how many people were living here. Thirty families? Forty? It was hard to be sure. A big gathering, certainly.

By bringing her hostage here, Milka Rosic had put them all at risk.

Barely twenty minutes had passed since Charlie had handed Javor Milos over to his Edinburgh colleagues. The assassin had given them no trouble. When Charlie had read him his rights, he hadn't said a word.

'I know you speak English,' he said, as he heaved Milos to his feet. 'So I'll assume you understood what I just said.'

Mute, Milos looked right through him. His hands were blue with cold, his face was drawn. Charlie knew how he felt.

As soon as he was confident Milos was neutralised, he called Brian Burfield to tell him the good news. His boss got in there first, with news of Dunja's safe arrival at the Parliament building.

'Well done, Charlie,' Brian said. He sounded as happy as a man who'd just lost his winning lottery ticket. 'But you're only halfway there. Milka Rosic is still very much at large.'

'Tell me something I don't know.'

'I've just heard from Nick Luard,' Brian went on. 'As soon as the name "Rosic" came up, he started taking an interest again. Milka Rosic has been known to MI6 for some time—as you can imagine. I've never seen Luard so excited. I think he's keen to get her into one of his interrogation suites.'

'I'll bet he is.'

'The upshot is, thanks to Luard and his friends in the Cabinet Office, there's a Special Forces team right behind you. They should be less than ten minutes away by now.'

Charlie thought about this. 'Okay. Look, Brian. Do what you can to stop them rushing in. We still don't know what Rosic is up to. Dunja might appear unharmed but we don't know what other cards she's getting ready to play. There could be other hostages. And she's almost certainly armed. There're a lot of innocent people in that camp. The last thing we need is the SAS bulldozing in and sparking something off. At least I just look like a harmless copper.'

'I'll do what I can. But there's a lot of momentum behind this now, Charlie. A lot of people are suddenly very interested in what you're doing up there.'

'I'm sure they are. But as far as I'm concerned—and until you tell me otherwise, Brian—this is still SOD business.'

'Agreed. Keep talking to me, Charlie. And be careful.'

Neutralising Milos had given Charlie the boost he needed. *One down, one to go.* Once he got inside the camp, however, he started wondering if this was such a good idea. There were so many hiding places, and he'd already seen what Rosic had achieved with a tiny pen-knife.

Maybe I should wait for the SAS after all.

The door to one of the caravans swung open. A woman stood just inside the threshold. She was drying her hands on a patterned cloth. She looked like somebody's grandmother. When he reached the foot of the steps, Charlie nodded a greeting.

'Morning,' he said. 'I'd like to take a look around, if I may.'

The old woman said nothing, just retreated and shut

the door. One of the boys looped his bike round Charlie, skidded to a halt and blew a raspberry. There was a bark behind him. When Charlie turned round, he saw a knot of people had gathered—one casually held the straining leash of a vicious-looking mongrel. There was some Rottweiler in there, for sure.

'Good morning,' he said, as firmly as possible.

'What d'you want?' said a young man at the front of the little crowd. Despite the cold, he was wearing just a T-shirt and shorts. 'We're here legal, you know.'

'I never said you weren't.'

'Muskers came yesterday. Said we're kushti.'

'I'm not here about that. I'm a police officer.' Those words didn't seem to instil confidence, and the men looked at each other. Even the dog seemed to bare its teeth a little more. 'I've come to warn you.'

''Bout what?' said an older man at the back of the crowd.

Charlie pointed up the hill. 'We've just arrested a man up there. He was carrying a high velocity rifle with a telescopic sight. The rifle was aimed right at your camp.'

The crowd stirred. The older man whispered something to a girl, who ran off behind one of the caravans.

'Why should we believe you?' said the young man in the T-shirt.

'Why would I lie?' Charlie replied.

'What's anyone want to shoot at us for?'

'That's what I'm here to find out.'

He wondered how many of them knew about Milka Rosic. She must have had at least one person on the inside, maybe more.

'I need to conduct a search,' he said. 'We believe there's a woman hiding here. A very dangerous woman. She probably entered your camp some time last night.

Did any of you notice any strangers? Any unusual comings or goings? A Jaguar?'

His gaze was met with blank stares. Those who wouldn't look at him kept their eyes on the ground. He wanted to shout at them, tell them he wasn't playing games.

But it wouldn't help.

'All right,' he said. 'I'm going to take a look around. If any of you remembers anything, come and talk to me…'

'Nobody said you could do a search,' said the young man. 'You got a warrant?'

'Look,' Charlie said, 'I didn't come here for an argument. I've come because I believe you're in danger. All of you. All I want to do is get to this woman before she starts making trouble for you. Trust me—the kind of trouble she makes is not the kind you want to get mixed up in.'

'Trust you?' said the old man. 'Without a warrant? Why should we?'

'Man on the hill wasn't the only one with a gun.' The young man was eyeing the Glock in Charlie's holster. 'Maybe you're the one bringing trouble.'

'We're here legal,' said a waif-like girl. She clung to the young man's arm. She looked scared.

The girl's fear was something he could use.

'Shall I tell you some of the things this woman's done?' said Charlie. He looked straight at the girl. 'Last year she sent a letter bomb to the home of a minor official in the Croatian government. The package was opened by the official's nine year-old daughter, who thought it was a birthday present. When it exploded, it blew both her hands off. Do you want to hear more?'

'Be quiet, musker,' growled the young man. 'Don't you go scaring folk.'

'You should be scared,' Charlie persisted, not taking

his eyes off the girl. 'She's here. I know she is. All I need to know is where she spent the night.'

The young man started hustling the girl out of the crowd, but not before she'd glanced into the depths of the camp. Charlie followed her eyes..

At the end of the makeshift street stood a caravan a little different from its neighbours. It was longer, lower, with silver sides and a charcoal-grey roof.

All the curtains were closed.

He started walking towards it. His knee still throbbed. He ignored the pain. The bicycle boys followed until the old man called them back with a low, barking command. Charlie passed a woman about to empty a bowl of water out of her door; when she saw him, she scowled and shrank inside.

When he was twenty metres away from the silver caravan, one of the curtains twitched. Instinct moved his legs faster. Only too aware he was surrounded by potential casualties, he drew his gun. He'd know Rosic the instant he saw her. He had no doubt she'd be armed. Having the Glock in his hand could make all the difference.

Take it easy. It might not be her.

But he knew it was.

Ten metres away. Behind him, somebody shouted. He ignored them. Five metres.

The caravan door swung slowly open.

Charlie had reached the bottom of the steps. He stopped. In the caravan's shadowy interior stood a woman with wide shoulders. *Swimmer's shoulders*, thought Charlie. The woman stepped on to the top step, into the light. The woman from the Interpol photofit, from the Stansted cameras. She wore a red cardigan over a white blouse which was missing several buttons. Her hair and eyes were dark. On her left cheek was the shadow of a bruise. It was Milka Rosic.

Charlie raised the Glock. In her right hand, Rosic was holding a small, black object.

'Drop the gun,' Charlie said. 'Drop it now.'

'It's not a gun,' said Rosic. Her English was lightly accented, husky and clipped.

Charlie let his eyes inspect the object. She wasn't lying. It wasn't a gun.

'Drop it anyway,' said Charlie. 'Now.' He moved forwards, towards her.

A smile played on Rosic's lips as she angled it towards him. It looked for all the world like a walkie-talkie.

'I suppose you wish to tell me I am under arrest,' said Rosic. 'Before you do that, let me tell you something.'

'Drop that,' said Charlie. 'Whatever it is. Drop it now!'

'I don't think so.'

Charlie was standing with one foot on the scrubby ground and the other on the caravan's bottom step. Both hands were locked on his gun, which was pointing straight at Rosic's chest. He couldn't shoot her, not if she was unarmed. He backed up two paces.

'Put it down and walk slowly down the steps.'

Rosic didn't move.

'I'm going to count to three,' said Charlie.

'I'm sure you are. But if you do, know this: before you reach "two" I will push this.' Rosic stroked her thumb across a silver button on the device. 'Do you want to know what happens when I push this button?'

'I'm not going to play games with you …'

Rosic descended to the next step down. Charlie's finger tightened on the trigger. He was so fucking close. *Calm down, Charlie*, he told himself.

'Standard issue Glock 17.' Rosic tilted her head. 'Every policeman's favourite. When you put two and a half kilograms on the trigger, I take a 9mm bullet in the chest. How much are you pulling now, policeman? One kilogram? One and a half?'

Is she carrying a gun? I can't see one. What the hell is that thing she's holding?

She was on the next step down. Charlie didn't want to back away but barely a metre separated her from the muzzle of his gun. He needed room to move if she decided to jump him. She made the decision for him by stopping there.

'I will—how do you say it?—put you out of the misery.' She held out the device. 'This is a radio transmitter. The same as you might use to control a model aeroplane. But simpler. With this, there is only one control.'

'You can't get away,' Charlie said. 'We have the whole camp surrounded.'

Her demeanour changed. Heavy eyebrows dropped low; her voice dropped lower still. 'I believe you,' she growled. 'Now it is time for you to believe me. This button controls a detonator. The detonator is attached to ten pounds of plastic explosive. The plastic explosive is attached to a belt. Can you guess what the belt is attached to, mister policeman with a gun? Or rather, *who* it is attached to?'

Charlie's stomach went into freefall. He felt his finger increase the pressure on the trigger. Two kilograms, he heard Rosic say in his head. If he shot her in the arm, would that be enough? *What if I miss?* He willed his finger to relax, felt the trigger relax with it.

'Yes, you can guess. I see it in your eyes. So let me confirm what you suspect. The belt with the explosives is attached very firmly round the waist of our esteemed

Foreign Minister, Hazbi Dunja. If you force me to push this button, the belt will explode and very many people will die. Most of them will die with small pieces of Hazbi Dunja embedded inside them like shrapnel. There will be a very large mess, followed quickly by very large headlines. So, I suggest you put your little gun away and join me inside.'

She started retreating up the steps, back into the caravan. Charlie tried to move his legs, but they wouldn't obey. In his hand, the Glock suddenly felt heavy … and useless. But what other weapon did he have?

Rosic reached round the door frame to fiddle with something inside the caravan, something Charlie couldn't see. She didn't take her eyes off his. The movement made the lapels of her torn blouse fall open, revealing the expanse of bare skin below her throat.

Táchiben. The word jumped unbidden into Charlie's head.

'What happened to your pendant?' he snapped.

Rosic stopped. For the first time she looked unsettled. 'What do you mean?' she said.

'It looks to me like someone tried to rip your blouse off. Is that how you lost it? I see there's some dried blood behind your ear. Did it come from the man whose throat you cut? You should be more careful about washing yourself.'

She snarled—actually snarled. *Like a tiger.* Her teeth were tiny and looked very white.

'What do you know of this?'

'We found the pendant lying on the kitchen floor of a shabby house in Leeds. Exactly where you dropped it. Careless to lose something you treasure so much, don't you think?'

Rosic's thumb tensed on the button. The tendons in her wrist stood out like cords.

'You think I won't do it?' she shouted. Suddenly her other hand was holding a switchblade. She twisted her finger and the blade snapped into view. 'Let me prove what I will do!'

She slashed the knife twice across her arm, just below the elbow, opening deep red gashes. Blood first oozed, then poured down her arm to her wrist. Soon her whole forearm was painted red; slowly her hand began to turn red, too.

'I am not afraid!' she said, brandishing the switchblade in one hand, the transmitter in the other. Runnels of blood covered the latter; as she waved her hand, red droplets hissed through the sunlight. 'Kill me or not, I do not care. But if you make me a martyr, I will make many martyrs of my own. Then their blood will be on your hands. Here—this it what it will feel like!'

She flicked her wrist, and blood sprayed through the air. Several drops landed on the back of Charlie's hand. He flinched, but didn't move the gun aside. He could shoot her now, in the heart, in the head, finish this business once and for all. She was armed, a legitimate target.

'You won't push that button,' he said. 'If you were going to push it, you'd have done it already. What is it you want?'

Rosic narrowed her eyes. 'Now, at least, you ask a sensible question. You ask what I want. Very well, I will show you. Come inside with me now.'

'No. No way. We stay out here or…'

Rosic bared her teeth. 'Do you want to make the headlines, policeman?'

He couldn't afford to take the chance. And she knew it.

Charlie let out a faltering sigh. Lowering his gun, he climbed the steps and went inside the caravan.

Milka Rosic kicked the door shut behind him.

With the curtains drawn, it was gloomy. Charlie just could make out tiny cabinets packed with china and silverware. Flowery cushions sat plumped on plush seats. It all looked disconcertingly domestic.

A light was flickering. Not a lamp but an old portable TV, perched on the narrow kitchen worktop. It was this that Rosic had reached for while she'd been standing in the doorway. Now she was standing beside it, adjusting the volume. Charlie edged towards her. Perhaps, while her guard was down…

His shin hit something hard. Looking down, he saw two small stools—like milking stools. Rosic had positioned them to form a makeshift barrier. Nothing he couldn't kick aside. But enough to slow him down.

'My thumb is still on the button,' she said, not even bothering to look at him. 'Do you really want to kill all those people?'

'Do you?' He could smell Rosic's blood. Her hand was black in the half-light. Blood dripped down the transmitter and on to the thin carpet.

'Shut up!' she said. 'And watch the television! If you do that, you may save many lives.'

'I don't believe you.'

Suddenly furious, Rosic hurled the switchblade down the length of the caravan. It stuck in the window frame at the far end, quivering. Now she had both hands on the transmitter. She was holding it out, aiming it straight at Charlie, as if he were the one she wanted to terminate. He heard a faint and dreadful squelching sound as her fingers slithered in her own blood.

'Let us do it then!' she screamed. The transmitter was trembling, *she* was trembling all over. 'Let us end it now! Do you think I have anything to lose? Do you think I care about this little man's life, about *any* of their lives?'

Her thumbs came down together, slipping in the blood, on to the button. Charlie saw it begin to depress, actually *heard* the button begin its descent into the transmitter's casing.

'Stop!' he shouted. Rosic froze, except for her hands, which continued to tremble. Her thumbs, bunched on the button, froze too. 'Stop! All right, you win. I'm in here now, I'm all yours. Tell me what you want. Then we can talk. Just don't push that button.'

Slowly, she lowered the transmitter.

'I don't need to tell you anything at all,' she said, softly, and pointed at the television. 'He does. Watch.'

The TV showed an image from one of the cameras inside the Scottish Parliament's grand debating chamber. The chamber was crowded, its great horseshoe of seats packed with Scottish MPs and other dignitaries. Likewise, the public and press galleries were full.

In front of them all, tiny beneath the soaring roof beams but dominating the proceedings nonetheless, stood Hazbi Dunja. He'd just started his speech.

'...so many years of persecution, the time has come to set history on a new course.' Dunja's voice echoed through the chamber. The audience listened in silence. When the camera cut to a close-up, Charlie saw that Dunja was exhausted. Shadows rimmed his eyes; his brow glistened. The hand in which he held his typewritten notes was trembling.

No wonder, thought Charlie, *given what's strapped to his stomach*!

Seated behind Dunja was a small group of people.

When the camera cut to a wide view, Charlie was able to pick out Scottish First Minister Andrew Molloy and his wife, Fiona. There were other faces he recognised but the one his eyes were drawn to belonged to the woman standing at the end of the line. She was standing stiff and alert, hands behind her back, eyes busy, scanning the chamber for trouble.

It was Alex.

She, like the rest of the platform party, was less than five metres from the bomb.

'The Balkan states,' Dunja continued, 'have a poor record concerning the treatment of ethnic minorities. Nowhere is this more apparent than in the Roma community. Nor is Croatia any different to its neighbours. Throughout our country and others, Romas are forced to live in squalor in city dumps or industrial wastelands. They cannot find employment. They are refused healthcare by doctors and nurses who treat them like animals. When they are driven out of the ghettos they live in, they have nowhere to go. Their men are beaten, their women are abused, their children fall ill and die. All this happens in a world that is supposed to be civilised. In a country that is supposed to be civilised. It is a situation that cannot be allowed to continue…'

Dunja faltered. Behind him, Andrew Molloy looked as if he'd just been asked to swallow a hippopotamus. Taking a silk handkerchief from his top pocket, Dunja wiped his brow. He looked up from his notes, straight at the camera. He opened his mouth, about to speak. But no words came out. He closed his mouth and lowered his notes. A low murmur started to rise from the audience.

In the caravan, Milka Rosic clenched her hands around

the transmitter. On the screen, Dunja mopped his brow a second time. Charlie tensed his muscles. Could he get past the stool barricade, knock the transmitter from her grip before she hit the button?

Dunja looked once more at the camera. Then he started speaking again, and Rosic relaxed.

'This is why I call for change. Not just change in Croatia, but in the international community as a whole. I have chosen to deliver this speech today, here in Scotland, because I believe the Scottish people understand, more than most, the principles at stake here. I believe their history is something from which we in my country can learn.

'Three hundred years ago, Scotland was a kingdom in its own right. It had its own Parliament, its own laws. When it was absorbed into what we know today as the United Kingdom, the Scots wanted to retain that Parliament. The English refused. Now, at last, the Scottish people have regained at least a little of their former independence. They have their Parliament back. They have won back the right to be free.

'What the Roma people of Croatia want is not so very different: they, too, want recognition of their freedom. I have listened to their arguments for many years. But only now do I understand. And only now am I in a position to do something about it.

'It therefore gives me great…pride…' again Dunja wiped his handkerchief across his brow, '…to announce the beginning a new era of tolerance in Croatia. Starting today, the rights of all Roma people to live and compete as equals within our country will be robustly upheld by the law. Just as the people of Scotland are able to assert their individuality, so the Roma people of Croatia will now be encouraged to assert theirs.'

As Dunja spoke, Rosic mouthed the words. This was her speech. With his translator in hospital in Zagreb, Dunja was the translator now, delivering Rosic's words to the audience. Rosic was captivated by the image on the screen. The bloody hand holding the transmitter had dropped to her side. As Dunja concluded his address— and the audience sat in stunned silence, rapidly followed by a rising thunder of applause—Charlie began to edge round the stools. The cheering rattled the TV set's cheap speaker. The camera switched to a bemused Andrew Molloy rising to shake Dunja's hand. In the background, Alex was visible, clearly eager to escort the Croatian Foreign Minister off the platform.

Charlie pressed his leg against the nearer of the two stools, ready to push it aside. Ready to pounce.

The TV went dead. In the sudden darkness, Rosic was just a silhouette, outlined against the dim glow of the curtains. She backed out of the kitchen and into the sitting area, still brandishing the transmitter.

'It's over,' said Charlie. 'It's done. He's done what you wanted. Now put that thing down and we can talk about it.'

'Yes, it is done,' she said, quietly. 'But it isn't over. If you want to talk, here is something we can talk about. Give me a reason, policeman—a good reason. Tell me why Hazbi Dunja shouldn't die anyway.'

29

March 2nd
09:36
Scottish Parliament, Edinburgh

THE APPLAUSE from the debating chamber had died down. Henry flashed his pass at a security guard and hurried round to the back of the platform. He could just see the heads of the speakers as they made their way backstage. Dunja, being tall, and with that dreadful comb-over, stood out clearly in the throng. Behind him, wearing a shell-shocked smile, was Andrew Molloy. Right at his side, still taking her bodyguard role very seriously, was Alex Chappell.

Henry had been as astonished as everyone else by Hazbi Dunja's speech. Such an about-face. And to put his own government on the spot like that: the Predsjednik would be furious.

They'll have to see it through, thought Henry, in wonder. *Such a public arena…they'll have no choice but to stand by Dunja's every word.*

He could imagine the shockwaves beating through the Croatian bureaucracy. Somewhere in Zagreb, one of his counterparts was watching a series of walls come crashing down. And no doubt wondering how the hell to spin it so the Predsjednik came out looking good.

On the subject of spin, Henry wondered if there was a way he could use the controversial content of the address to turn things around for the department. He could almost hear his report to Oliver Fleet now:

'Clearly Dunja knew there would be people who wanted to stop him making such a radical speech. It's likely he was planning to slip UK security all along. We couldn't possibly have anticipated such a hidden agenda. Nor, without full sight of the text of his speech, could we have known he would attract the attention of such dangerous individuals as Javor Milos and Milka Rosic.'

Okay, it needed some work. But it had a ring, if not of truth, then at least of plausibility. Given that Oliver's neck was one of those it would save, Henry thought he'd go along with it.

Talk about Lady Luck. The day just kept getting better and better.

The Croatian Foreign Minister was descending the steps leading out of the chamber. To Henry's surprise, as soon as Dunja reached the bottom, he made straight for him. Molloy and some of his cronies tried to follow, but Dunja muttered something to Alex, who held up her arm to keep them back.

'You meet me outside,' Dunja said to Henry.

'Yes, I was there when you arrived,' Henry replied.

'You are security?'

'I, er, well, not exactly.'

'I see you with the policewoman, outside. You arrange things?'

'I am pleased to say…' Henry puffed out his chest, '…that I was indeed instrumental in arranging your visit to the United Kingdom. In fact, the complete itinerary for your Scottish…'

'When you hear what I am going to say,' hissed Dunja, 'you will no longer be pleased.'

Henry suddenly felt out of his depth. Something in Dunja's eyes bothered him. He looked round at Alex, saw she'd been joined by a tanned, bald man with a walkie-talkie. They were talking in whispers. Both were studying Dunja intently.

'Sergeant Chappell,' Henry called, 'I wonder if you could…'

But she was already heading his way, with the bald man close behind. He was muttering into his walkie-talkie. Seconds later, four security men descended on the platform party and started ushering them back up the steps.

'Mr Dunja,' Chappell said, 'this is Jim Connelly. He's in charge of security here at Holyrood.'

'Security,' said Dunja. 'Yes, good!' Gripping her shoulders, he said, 'You must take me out of this building. You must help me.'

'Really, Mr Dunja…' Henry began.

'Shut up!' Dunja glared at him, then turned back to Alex. 'Listen to me. Listen very well. The woman I travel with. She is not Jelenka Levnicki. She is…'

'We know who she is, sir,' said Alex, quietly.

Dunja blinked. 'Good. You have good intelligence. But there is something you don't know.'

'What's going on?' snapped Henry. Dunja's behaviour

was disturbing him. Now they were back on schedule he was keen to keep the momentum going.

Several corridors led away from the backstage area. Dunja turned to the nearest one, beckoning them to follow. The corridor was empty.

'Here,' he said, 'where nobody will see.'

In silence, he opened the jacket he'd kept buttoned since getting out of the Mercedes. Then he pulled his shirt out of his trousers and lifted it up to the level of his nipples. His stomach was swathed in black gaffer tape. Under the tape, at regular intervals round his waist, Henry saw a series of flat packages. Dunja turned round to reveal a small black box—about the size of a pack of cigarettes—taped in the small of his back. Six wires ran out of the box and under the tape.

'Is that a…' Henry began, his voice pitched slightly higher than normal.

Dunja gave him a withering look, dropped his shirt and turned round again. 'You must take me away from here.'

Chappell and Connelly shared a look.

'That bomb's big enough to blow a sizeable hole in pretty much anything within a fifty metre radius,' Alex said, calmly. 'We need to get Mr Dunja into an enclosed space—minimum collateral damage.'

'Uh, do you really think it will come to that?' said Henry.

'Yes,' said Alex. 'We have to act fast. There isn't much time.'

Collateral damage? thought Henry. He felt himself blanche, with a sudden vision of the pristine walls of Holyrood splattered with blood. Not just any old blood either: his blood.

'Go along the corridor, and take the stairs to the basement level,' said Connelly, gesturing over his shoulder.

'There's a half-finished antechamber that will be empty.'
He spun away and immediately got on his walkie-talkie:
'This is Connelly. Security bulletin, code one. Evacuate
the Parliament building and assemble at fire rendezvous
points. All personnel respond and act immediately.
Repeat, code one security alert, assemble…'

Henry discovered his mouth was flapping open.
Suddenly things felt grossly unfair. He couldn't think of
a single thing to say.

'Did she make you deliver that speech?' asked
Chappell, as she began to usher Hazbi Dunja along the
corridor at a quick pace. Her voice was low and steady.
Henry felt like screaming, dragged behind like a toddler
on an invisible cord.

Dunja nodded. 'She wrote it. She tells me I must
speak it, word by word. If I do not say everything she
has written…'

Henry didn't know whether to stay or go. In the end
he followed.

'She smuggles a gun on the aeroplane. She threatens
to shoot me in the taxi cab—that is when she first reveals
herself to me. She shoots the radio in the taxi and tells
the driver not to stop or he will die. He obeys.'

'And you obeyed, too?' said Alex. She was close to
Dunja. *Shielding him*, thought Henry.

'What choice do I have? I have been weak with influenza. I wait for a good moment. When we escape from
the house in Leeds, then I think I will escape from her.'

'What happened?'

Dunja shrugged. 'Somewhere she lost her gun. But in the
house she finds another. She hits me on the head with it.
Then she drives the car here. Each time I wake up, she hits
me again. She is a ruthless woman. But please, the bomb…'

At the door to the stairs, marked 'John Smith Conference Room', Henry paused, and Connelly went past him. There was something unnatural about entering that…cell…with a human bomb. He could almost hear Hazbi Dunja ticking.

'I, er, suppose I'll have to leave it with you, then. After all—you're the experts.'

'Yes, we are.' said Chappell. She looked back at Henry—no, *past* him. 'Although there is something you could do.'

Henry's airline breakfast heaved in his stomach. He felt both cold and feverish. He just wanted to run…and run and run. But the worst thing of all was that, beneath his terror, he was thinking only this: *I arranged for Hazbi Dunja to come to this country. So if anyone's responsible for him, I am.*

'What?' he said, through a mouth that felt full of cotton wool.

Alex pointed back into the corridor. 'Have a word with him.'

Henry looked. There, standing with his arms folded and his face red, was Andrew Molloy.

'Do you mind telling me,' said the Scottish First Minister, 'what the hell is going on in my Parliament.'

30

March 2ⁿᵈ
09:37
Holyrood Park, Edinburgh

'YOU'VE done what you came for,' said Charlie. 'It's time to stop.'

'He is a killer! He has the blood of my people on his hands.'

'And you've turned the tables on him. Think about it! Isn't he worth more to you alive? If you kill him now, the speech he's given on your behalf becomes meaningless.'

'Not meaningless. The words are spoken. They cannot be unsaid. The wind has already changed. Whether he is alive or dead, it no longer matters. Hazbi Dunja's life is worth nothing now.'

Rosic's thumb touched the button.

The caravan's interior lit up. Something punched Charlie backwards. The whole world was white-hot. An image flashed before his dazzled eyes: the Range Rover in the service station lifting off the ground as the petrol tank exploded. His shoulder hit one of the narrow cabinets. China rained past him, smashing on the floor. His ears felt like they did when he dived too deep in the swimming pool near his Bayswater flat.

Charlie's first thought was that Rosic's bomb had gone off. But that made no sense. The bomb was round Dunja's waist, not here in the camp.

An explosion. But what blew up? A gas canister?

Reeling forward, away from the wall, he saw one of the windows was broken. There was movement outside. Movement inside too: something rolling on the thin carpet, spewing smoke…

Stun grenade!

Still struggling to balance—to see even—he sought out Rosic. His eyes were streaming. He could hear nothing but a dull roar. At last he spotted her, staggering about just like he was. She still had hold of the transmitter, but by the antenna now.

Did she push the button?

Charlie lunged forward. Rosic was spinning towards him. He threw himself against her. Already off-balance, she fell sideways. He fumbled for her wrists, grasped them hard. The blood made them slippery; he fought to keep his grip. He tried to straddle her, to force her arms down to the floor, but she brought her knee up into his groin. Charlie couldn't stay on his feet and folded, his hands automatically dropping to his testicles. She rolled on top of him, tried to bring her knee up again. He twisted his hips to throw her off. She held on, but at least he'd deflected the blow. Spitting, small teeth bared, she lunged at his face, trying to bite. The bloody fingers of her right hand were busy, trying to flip the transmitter so she could reach the button. Charlie thrust out his arm and pounded her hand against the wooden corner of the couch, trying to force her to release her grip.

The caravan door burst open. A black-clad SAS officer rushed up the steps. At the same moment, Milka Rosic finally pulled her left wrist free from Charlie's fingers. She fumbled for the transmitter, which she was holding in her other hand. The SAS man's hand closed on her collar. He heaved her off Charlie, threw her sideways. Charlie rolled with her, bleary eyes tracking her hands through the smoke. Her empty hands...

Where is it?

Rosic's leg came up again. She was impossibly nimble.

The toe of her boot hit the tip of the SAS man's jaw. His eyes rolled white and he fell, dead weight, on top of Charlie. Rosic scrambled clear, tripped, picked herself up. She crouched, poised and feral, hands like black claws, white smoke from the grenade boiling round her, casting her eyes around, doing exactly what Charlie was doing.

Looking for the transmitter.

31

March 2nd
09:37
Scottish Parliament, Edinburgh

HENRY Worthington hovered for a moment and took Andrew Molloy by the arm. *Only too happy to be getting away.*

'First Minister…' Alex heard his voice disappear as Connelly shut the door.

She turned to Jim Connelly and Dunja. Just the three of them. Her mouth was dry; her thoughts felt two sizes too big for her head. She swallowed down her fear.

'The room's down here,' said Connelly. 'It's empty, about to be redecorated. It should be big enough.'

The antechamber turned out to be a large conference room. At the far end, dustsheets covered a mountain of stacking chairs. Along one wall stood paint-spattered ladders. The room had no windows.

'Basement level,' said Connelly. 'We're surrounded by several thousand tons of good Scottish bedrock.'

'Let's hope we don't need it,' said Alex.

Dunja was standing, dazed, like a lost child. She took

his hand and led him to the middle of the room. His palms, like hers, were cold and slick with sweat. They stood like mis-matched dancers waiting for the music to begin.

Here we go...

'As I see it,' Alex said, 'we've got two choices. It all depends on how volatile we think Rosic is.'

'She's gone this far,' said Connelly. 'We have to assume the worst.'

'Well,' she went on, 'our first option is simply to keep Mr Dunja isolated. Charlie's on his way into the travellers' camp—if he isn't there already. He might have some news for us about Rosic soon. And Special Forces have been alerted. She might already be in custody.'

'Or she might be getting ready to blow up the bomb,' said Dunja. He raised a trembling hand to his chest, as if to touch the bomb, then thought better of it.

'Yes,' said Alex, 'she might. And as long as we're waiting, we're helpless.'

Dunja backed away from her. He looked suddenly taller, more assured. 'You speak of isolation,' he said. 'As long as the two of you stand next to me, I am not isolated. You all should go. If my time has come...then that is the way of things.'

Alex took a deep breath. 'Well,' she said, 'that leads me to our second option. We stay here with Mr Dunja and I try to deactivate the bomb.'

Connelly nodded.

'Do you know what you are doing?' said Dunja.

Chappell caught the chauvinism in his tone, but ignored it.

'I'm an SOD officer with a job to do,' she said. 'I'm responsible for the safety of a visiting diplomat, who's enjoyed precious little security during his visit to our country so far. I intend to redress the balance.'

She broke off. Close up, she could smell the stale sweat on Dunja's skin.

'Go, Jim,' she said softly. 'Thanks for your help but…I don't think you can do any good down here.'

Connelly looked at her, gave a little smile.

'They send us Jocks on courses too, Alex,' Connelly replied. 'You know as well as I do, this could take two of us.'

He frowned. She'd never seen such bushy brows on a man with no hair. The eyes they framed looked tired and haunted.

'I'll bet you wish you'd stayed on holiday now,' she said, circling Dunja. *You made a name for yourself with letter bombs, Milka Rosic,* she thought to herself. *How are you at scaling up?*

'Nah,' Connelly replied. 'The place was dull as ditch-water. Great place to retire to, but it's not what I'd call buzzing.'

Motioning Dunja to keep still, Alex eased off his jacket. Then she unbuttoned his cuffs and removed his shirt.

'If the circumstance was different,' said Dunja, nervously, 'it would please me to be undressed by a pretty girl.'

'I'm sure it would, sir.'

'Did you really follow me here, all the way from Stansted airport?'

'Yes, sir, I did. With my partner, Charlie Paddon.'

She circled Dunja again. Most of his torso was strapped with gaffer tape.

'You are devoted to your duty,' said Dunja.

'Just doing my job, sir.'

'Do you know why Javor Milos wanted to kill me?'

'Not really, sir, no.'

'What would you say if I told it was because of something I did in the war? Something terrible. Something, perhaps, that I deserve to die for.'

'I would say that while you're in this country, it's my job to protect you. If you die while I'm on duty, I've failed. I don't consider failure an option.'

'You are brave.'

'No, sir. Just stubborn. Now, tell me, do you consider Milka Rosic to be a volatile individual?'

Dunja frowned. 'A...volatile? What does this mean?'

'Will she push the button?'

'Yes.' No hesitation. 'Yes, she will.'

She beckoned Connelly over. 'How many wires do you see?'

'I count six.' One by one, Connelly traced the raised lines beneath the tape.

'Agreed. That probably means two live and four fake.'

'Fakes will be rigged to the battery. Pull the wrong one and they'll be peeling all three of us off the walls.'

'Roger that.'

Sweat was trickling into Alex's eyes. She brushed it away, wiped her shaking hands dry on her thighs. Between them, she and Connelly peeled away the top layers of tape. When the adhesive pulled at his skin, Dunja flinched. When Dunja flinched, they did too. Fear was contagious. Alex wondered how much the minister knew about explosives. He'd been a tank commander, after all.

Soon all the wires were exposed. Three were blue, three black. All ran into the small box containing the radio receiver. To make the bomb safe, all they had to do was cut one of the two live wires. Cutting one of the four fakes would detonate the explosives.

Alex's chest felt full of machinery. Incredible how the human heart could beat so fast and not explode.

She took a deep breath. In. Hold. Out. Studied the wires. Forced herself to concentrate.

On the face of it, the odds were poor. On the other hand, this whole thing looked like a rush job. The booby trap was a token effort. If they kept their heads, defusing it should be no problem.

But there was someone she had to talk to before they got started.

She dropped her head, closed her eyes.

Fraser? Can you hear me? I know you're there. I know every good boy can hear his mummy's thoughts. So listen carefully. I've got to work late again. I have to do something very important. It's to do with the goodies and the baddies. When you're older, maybe I'll tell you about it. So be good for Danni, and eat all your vegetables. I promise I'll be home tomorrow night to read you a bedtime story.

I promise.

She took a deep breath. If only she could talk to Lawrie like that, ask him if he'd booked that table yet, tell him there was no way she was going to miss dinner with her gorgeous husband. But, given how hopeless he was with his mobile phone, she thought telepathy was probably asking too much.

'Are you sure you know what you are doing, miss?' said Dunja as she gently traced the wires with her fingers. 'Would it not be better to wait for your SAS friends?'

'Milka Rosic won't wait,' Alex replied. 'Besides, I have a date this evening. Jim—give me a hand here.'

Where are you, Charlie? she thought.

32

March 2nd
09:38
Holyrood Park, Edinburgh

WHITE smoke boiled against the caravan ceiling. Gasping for breath, Charlie shoved the unconscious SAS man off his chest. It felt like hours had passed since he'd burst in, but it could only have been seconds. He could hear more footsteps on the steps.

Rosic, too, heard the other soldiers approaching. She whirled, pulled open the drawers of a cabinet one by one. The drawers crashed on to the couch, spilling papers and cutlery. The third yielded a pistol. She snatched it up. Then she stopped.

Charlie followed her gaze. The transmitter was teetering on the edge of the couch. Rosic made a grab for it. As she stretched, Charlie kicked out. He caught the backs of her knees and she folded up. She crashed to the floor and the transmitter slipped off the couch. Charlie opened his hand, extended his arm. The transmitter landed in his palm.

Instinctively, he clutched it. His fingers slithered over

the casing, sticky with blood. His thumb clenched the transmitter a centimetre short of the button.

Rosic scrabbled at his arm, fighting to get at the transmitter. She was waving the pistol like a club, having apparently forgotten its primary function. He ducked as she swung it at his face. It slammed into his shoulder. The second time he blocked her at the elbow, and the gun clattered onto the caravan floor.

From the door there came a series of shouts and thumps. The caravan rocked from side to side. Shadows juddered through the smoke. There was a sudden lull, like a silent intake of breath, then a single gunshot. Rosic collapsed without a sound, her mouth and eyes open, dark petals of blood unfurling across the front of her blouse. Her hands went limp, slipped from Charlie's sleeve.

Suddenly, the caravan was filled with men in camouflage and black balaclavas, shouting. They barged past Charlie, and descended on Rosic. One unloaded a pistol twice in her head. Charlie knew the drill—they had to be sure. As the ache in his balls subsided, and his head began to clear from the effects of the smoke grenade, he realised there were only three soldiers inside with him. He staggered to his feet and doubled up, coughing. The smoke still clawed at his throat. One of the SAS guys tried to take the transmitter off him. Charlie pushed him away.

'Need some air,' he mumbled, heading for the door. The man clapped him on the back.

Outside, the sun, newly risen above the trees, almost blinded him as he limped down the caravan steps. He couldn't stop rubbing his eyes, but as his vision cleared, anger set in. He couldn't believe how Special Forces had muscled in. They couldn't have known what was happening inside the caravan. They'd put everyone in danger—

not least, all the people back at Holyrood: Hazbi Dunja, all those around him…

Alex…

Behind Rosic's caravan was a yard of sorts. At least here he was away from the gaze of the travellers. In one corner, broken bicycles were heaped like steel knitting. Beside them were four brand new car tyres. Seagulls wheeled overhead.

He sat on one of the tyres and studied the transmitter. Had the button been pushed? There was no way of knowing. How could he tell if the bomb had gone off? He craned his neck, attempting to achieve the impossible and see over the top of Arthur's Seat and the Salisbury Crags. Would he see a plume of smoke rising into the sky?

That fucking idiot Luard! Trust him to send in a bunch of gung-ho Specials.

As his vision cleared, he saw the same knot of people who'd met him near the camp entrance, still watching, but hemmed in now by policemen. There were uniforms everywhere, it seemed, both police and Special Forces. White smoke drifted out through the door of the caravan, through the shattered window.

Gingerly, he put the transmitter down on the damp grass. He wished the thing had an on-off switch. The sooner it was deactivated the better. They'd all been on basic unexploded bomb courses as part of their SOD training, but Alex was the expert when it came to explosives.

Moving an arm that felt like it belonged to a robot—a robot that had been through a car crusher, at that—Charlie Paddon unclipped his radio. It looked disturbingly like Rosic's transmitter device. His fingers, caked in Rosic's blood, left visible prints on the plastic. He didn't care.

Hand trembling, he raised it to his mouth.

'Alex?' he said. 'Are you there?'

Static. He imagined the signal from his radio some-how causing the bomb to detonate. He shook himself, said again, 'Sergeant Alex Chappell. This is Charlie Paddon. Do you read me? Over.'

More static. Charlie watched the sunlight stroke the side of the caravan. The shadow of a seagull slid across the roof.

He tried one last time.

'Alex. Come in, Alex.'

A voice crawled through the static. 'Charlie? Is that you?'

'Alex?'

'Who else, you muppet! Are you all right? I was be-ginning to get worried.'

'Worried? About me? What about you? Are you okay?'

'Covered in gaffer tape, but otherwise just peachy. I'll tell you something. They don't make bombs like they used to.'

Charlie wanted to ask her if Hazbi Dunja was okay, if Brian Burfield knew what had happened, wanted to tell her he was proud of her for getting the explosives off Dunja without blowing them both to atoms. He wanted to tell her that Rosic was dead, that he'd shot Javor Milos and wrestled him to the ground and that the only thing the crazy assassin had wanted to take with him into cus-tody was a book about some guy on a winged horse. He wanted to tell her that the long chase was over, that their missing diplomat wasn't missing any more and that de-spite all the dominoes falling over yesterday, there was a whole row still standing today. Their man had delivered his speech—even if it wasn't quite the speech he'd in-tended to make—and stepped off the platform still breathing. Against all the odds, they'd done their jobs and caught their runaway.

'Knickers clean.'

'Just about,' laughed Alex.

'Fancy a drive down to London in a red BMW tomorrow?'

'Count me in. Just as long as you don't keep fiddling with that bloody seat.'

After he'd signed off, Charlie slipped off the tyre and sank to his knees. The ground was hard and the long grass was covered in dew. He rubbed his hands through the grass, washing them clean. From his pocket he drew the souvenir he'd bought in the Royal Armouries gift shop two years previously, when he'd still had a girl to call his own.

The little horned mask stared up at him, somehow sly. Charlie kissed it, gazed across to where the sun was soaring above the tree line and said a silent *thank you* to whoever might be listening to his thoughts. In front of the sun, herring gulls wheeled. On the breeze, he suddenly realised, he could smell the sea.

33

March 2nd
09:51
Scottish Parliament, Edinburgh

HENRY Worthington stared in the cloakroom mirror, calmed his breathing.

'We live to fight another day, my friend,' he said to his reflection, which smiled back with a somewhat lupine grin.

Henry smoothed down his Savile-tailored lapels, checked his flies again and straightened his tie. He even permitted himself a wink of satisfaction.

Andrew Molloy and his team were in the press suite. The press conference had been cancelled and the room was empty. No doubt there was a crowd of reporters gathered somewhere in the Holyrood complex, foaming at the mouth.

There goes the schedule again, thought Henry as he waved his pass at the security guards.

'Any news?' said Molloy, as Henry came up to him. 'My people want me out of the building, but I'm buggered if I'm running from my own Parliament.'

Henry was about to tell him getting out was probably

a very good idea. Could a diffused bomb still be a danger? Perhaps a turn in the gardens was what he needed.

The door to the press suite swung open, revealing a woman in police uniform, the bald security man with the suntan and the Croatian Foreign Minister. They were followed shortly after by a crowd of MPs, aides and security officers. For once, Henry was happy to let other people do the fussing. The rest of the day would be a complicated mix of rescheduled meetings, debriefings and general diplomatic shenanigans. He wouldn't be able to keep his head down for long, but right now there was a call he was dying to make.

Retreating to the corner of the room, he pulled out his mobile and dialled Nick Luard's direct line from memory. MI6 didn't like you keeping their number in your address book.

'You're through to Nick Luard's voicemail...' said a voice at the other end. Henry waited impatiently for the beep, then said,

'Worthington here. Nick, if you're…'

That was as far as he got before Luard picked up. 'What's the latest?' he said. His normally smooth tones were edged with something rougher. Henry hoped it was panic.

'You mean you don't know?' said Henry. 'I would have thought the SAS would keep you up to date.'

'I'm in no mood for games, Henry. Just tell me what's going on.'

'What's going on,' said Henry, 'is those charming people from Special Operations—Diplomats have managed not only to take out Javor Milos and Milka Rosic, but also to defuse the bomb that was strapped round the waist of our runaway diplomat. It seems we were right to place our trust in Chief Superintendent Burfield, after all.'

Luard hesitated for only a split-second before saying, 'Really? You didn't seem to find anyone trustworthy yesterday, Henry. Including Burfield's SODs.'

Henry smiled. Luard was good. 'I wouldn't worry yourself about that, Nick. If I were you, I'd start thinking about what you can do to reassure me this won't happen again. Let's meet tomorrow morning, my office. We can talk about how better to integrate the intelligence service into our overall diplomatic function. We'll make it an early start—how does eight o'clock sound?'

'It sounds fine, Henry.' Yes, definitely some gravel in the voice there. 'I'll look forward to it.'

He hung up. Jim Connolly was waving to him from the other side of the room. When he got an opportunity, he'd have to ask him where he went on holiday. That really was one hell of a tan.

Straightening his tie, he folded his mobile into his jacket pocket and joined the cluster of people round Hazbi Dunja. He shook hands and listened to what everyone had to say, even those who weren't talking to him. Especially those, in fact. The wheels were back on the wagon again, turning away, which meant Henry Worthington had work to do.

Someone had to keep everything oiled.

34

March 2nd
09:55
Holyrood Park, Edinburgh

WHEN Charlie stood, his knee ballooned with pain. He hobbled forward a few paces, wincing.

No gym for you this week, Chief Inspector Paddon, he told himself.

Picking up the transmitter, he limped back across the yard. It had come together in the end. But there was still work to be done. There always was.

Blocking his way back was the eldest of the three lads who'd escorted him into the Romany camp. The boy's hair was long and tousled; his eyes were vivid blue.

'Is she dead, mister?' he said, with relish

Charlie wasn't in the mood to share the enthusiasm. 'Yes,' he said. 'She's dead.'

The boy looked unimpressed, and wheeled his bike closer. 'What's that you got there?'

Charlie showed him. 'It's a remote control for an explosive device,' he said.

'You're shittin' me,' said the boy. 'They don't give you that stuff.' But his blue eyes were wide.

'No,' said Charlie, 'they don't. This isn't exactly police issue. I had to go through a lot to get my hands on it.'

'It's all covered in blood.'

'It's a long story.'

'So is it always like this? All remote thingies and blood and bombs and that?'

'Not always, no.'

'Still sounds pretty cool though.'

'I don't know about cool. But it's always interesting.'

'What's your name?' said the boy.

'Charlie Paddon. What's yours?'

'Eric.'

Charlie extended his hand. 'Nice to meet you, Eric. Take it easy.' They shook hands, then the boy started wheeling his bike away.

'You too, musker,' he said, as he skirted round the tyres and disappeared.

Charlie made his way out of the yard. There was plenty still to tie up in Edinburgh, but already London was calling. He thought of the old Clash song. He hadn't heard it for years. Funny, how it had just come into his head.

I'll phone DI Watts in Leeds, he decided. *Maybe he can get a driver to bring the BMW up here. We can escort Dunja back together then, me and Alex. I'll talk Dunja's chauffeur into taking the coast road.*

He wondered if they'd let him stop off along the way, so he could stand on the shore and look at the sea. It was a long time since he'd had his ocean fix. Just five minutes, that was all he needed.

After that, it would be back to business. He and Alex had a busy week ahead. Priority one was chaperoning Hazbi Dunja through the rest of his schedule and then, in two days' time, putting him safely on a Croatia Airlines plane, heading east. Let his own people worry about him for a while.

Though given what Dunja had said in his speech, 'worry' wasn't the word.

A breeze moved the trees and ruffled his hair. The last strands of cloud had shredded away, leaving clear, salt-scented air. Charlie took a deep breath, savouring the taste. He hoped DI Watts could swing the driver for him. There were a lot of miles ahead and only one satisfactory way to cover them. He was looking forward to getting back behind the wheel of the red car.

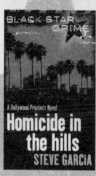

If you enjoyed this book, then make sure you also read other titles in the Black Star Crime™ series. Order direct and we'll deliver them straight to your door. Our complete titles list is available online.

www.blackstarcrime.co.uk

Book Title/Author	ISBN & Price	Quantity
Runaway Minister Nick Curtis	978 1 848 45000 4 £3.99	
Streetwise Chris Freeman	978 1 848 45001 1 £3.99	
A Narrow Escape Faith Martin	978 1 848 45002 8 £3.99	
Murder Plot Lance Elliot	978 1 848 45003 5 £3.99	
A Perfect Evil Alex Kava	978 1 848 45004 2 £3.99	
Double Cross Tracy Gilpin	978 1 848 45005 9 £3.99	
Tuscan Termination Margaret Moore	978 1 848 45006 6 £3.99	
Homicide in the Hills Steve Garcia	978 1 848 45007 3 £3.99	
Lost and Found Vivian Roberts	978 1 848 45008 0 £3.99	
Split Second Alex Kava	978 1 848 45009 7 £3.99	

Please add 99p postage & packing per book
DELIVERY TO UK ONLY

Post to: End Page Offer, PO Box 1780, Croydon, CR9 3UH

Please ensure that you include full postal address details. Please pay by cheque or postal order (payable to Reader Service) unless ordering online. Prices and availability subject to change without notice.

Order online at: www.blackstarcrime.co.uk

Allow 28 days for delivery.

You may receive offers from Harlequin Mills & Boon and other carefully selected companies. If you would prefer not to share in this opportunity, please write to The Data Manager, PO Box 676, Richmond, TW9 1WU.